Honey In The Rock

Cheryl Daniels Johnson

iUniverse, Inc.
Bloomington

Honey In The Rock

iUniverse books may be ordered through booksellers or by contacting:

iUniverse
1663 Liberty Drive
Bloomington, IN 47403
www.iuniverse.com
1-800-Authors (1-800-288-4677)

ISBN: 978-1-4697-4518-3 (sc)
ISBN: 978-1-4697-4519-0 (hc)
ISBN: 978-1-4697-4520-6 (e)

Printed in the United States of America

Library of Congress Control Number: 2012900618

iUniverse rev. date: 2/20/2012

Preface

❖ ❖ ❖

This book is dedicated to those who have a form of godliness but deny the power that God has given to them. The characters are fictional and based solely on my imagination and the creativity given to me by God. The only truth to the book is the Word of God and the principles of God that I have used.

I wrote this book to creatively explain the essential principles and practices of the Holy Spirit. My goal is to enlighten those who do not have an understanding of the essential principles of the Holy Spirit. My prayer is that this book will encourage people to operate in the power and the anointing of God—not just a weekly Sunday experience, but a life-changing relationship with God. Additionally, I pray that this book piques the interest of the reader to read the Word of God regarding the teaching of the Holy Spirit and find God's will through the power and anointing of the Holy Spirit.

Acknowledgments

❖ ❖ ❖

I thank my Lord and Savior Jesus Christ for giving me the vision, courage, and determination to complete this journey of letting go and letting God.

To my biggest fan, my husband, Hollis Johnson, I am forever grateful for your everlasting support, prayers, friendship, and love.

I could not have completed this project without the support of my family: to my sister, Rita Walker; her husband, Charles; and my niece and nephew, Brian Gregory and Katherine Nicole, thank you for believing when I did not believe.

To my eldest brother, Gregory Daniels; my beautiful sister-in-law, Cynthia; and my nephew, Emmanuel, I would like to thank you for consistently covering me in prayers throughout this entire journey.

To my big little brother who is my coach and exhorter, Anthony Daniels, and to his wonderful and gorgeous wife, Andrea, I would like to thank you for your prayers and words of wisdom that have covered me in times of need. To my newfound brother, Ralph McCoy, I would like to thank you for being an essential part of my journey and being a true believer of God's Word. I am grateful for having you in my life.

To my circle of dear friends: Jackie Davis Dozier, thank you for all the long distance calls and laughter. You are a true friend and supporter of this project. To my dear friend, Chimain Douglas, thank you for helping me carry the vision, always trusting in God for me, and believing in me.

To my dear friend, Laverne Marion Holston Blount, thank you for keeping me grounded and never forgetting the path we have taken together as childhood friends and adults. Thank you to Sylvia Yvette Wells for believing in me and for your prayers.

To my dear college buddies and friends, Beverly Terry Keaton, Valerie Hixon King, and Cynthia Chicago Waters, thank you for always being there through thick and thin.

To my big sister in Christ, Sylvia Waddell, thanks to you and your husband, Maurice Waddell, for the endless support and prayers. To my mentor and friend, Luretha O'Conner, thank you for all of your wisdom and support.

A special thank you to LaVonne Hester-Smith, Ph.D. for her editing and proofing skills used in the final production of this book.

A special thanks to Chimain Douglas Ministries. I would like to thank Pastor Douglas for her countless Bible studies and prayer services on teaching and imparting of the Holy Spirit. I am grateful for the studies and ministering of the Holy Spirit. I appreciate the teaching and the knowledge you have imparted into this book. Pastor Douglas can be contacted at:

4002 Hwy 78, Suite 530-227
Snellville, Georgia USA
(678) 580-3310
www.ChimainDouglasMinistries.com

I would like to thank Margaret Yancey for working with me on this project during your battle with cancer and enduring with me until the end. For that I am forever thankful to God. May God bless and keep you. I thank God for your healing, your endurance, and your heart of love.

Finally, to my life coach, Wallette V. McCall, thank you for stepping up to the plate and challenging me to finish what God had given to me. Your gifts of accountability proved to be priceless to the completion of this work. You have made this project a true success story and have given me much hope for my next project. Ms. McCall can be contacted at:

Another Level Coaching, LLC
Breakthrough Life Coaching for Women
P.O. Box 45
Tucker, GA 30085
(877) 976-5837
www.AnotherLevelCoaching.com
wallette@anotherlevelcoaching.com

Special Thanks

✤ ✤ ✤

Thank you for believing that I could achieve and complete this book. Each and every one of you sparked my vision to continue this project. I am forever grateful for your love, patience, and prayers. I pray that this book will truly bless you as much as you have blessed me. I'll be forever grateful to you for your endless support. May God bless you and keep you.

Marcia Brown
Irmia Beverly Stephen
Verda Colvin
Sylvia Clark
Delores Duncan
Flora Eatman
Stephanie Mills-Ehigh
Vicki Hutchins
Sheila Kelley
Dee Morgan
Corey Mia Peavey
Valerie Vannoy
Tracy Reddick

Chapter One

✤ ✤ ✤

THE WIND ROARED LIKE a hungry lion looking for its prey. One moment it was calm and the next moment a storm suddenly and boldly established itself. This was a typical summer day in Georgia. Two women moved about the inside of a mansion. Warmth was expressed throughout the rooms and love radiated throughout the home. The tour was about to end in the studio, and the owner and her guest could hear the roaring of the wind. Jessica had no doubt that this was a pop-up storm. It was fitting that her tour for the curious and avaricious Denise would end here with God's glory.

"What was that sound? Why is that chair rocking?" Denise whispered as she followed Jessica's every move. "It sounds like you left the window open."

"Maybe it's just the wind," Jessica responded.

"But the wind wasn't blowing when we entered your house, and there are no windows in this room!"

Two years earlier, Jessica had the room built as a studio without windows for lighting and privacy. The room was used for voiceovers, tapings, and training classes. The echoes gave Denise a strange feeling. Even as a child, the thought of a dark room frightened her. Denise was known for jumping on the backs of friends at any sign of danger, especially when it was dark. Denise held her purse and positioned herself as close to Jessica as she could get. Suddenly, a blurred vision of a cloud appeared and a warm sensation came over Denise. Jessica fell to her knees and immediately began to worship and praise God. Denise headed for the door and never looked back.

Jessica Holmes stayed on her knees for hours that Saturday evening, July 19, 2003. The petite, professional looking forty-five-year-old was a trainer and a consultant. Her parents had nicknamed her Honey because of her golden brown complexion and hazel eyes. She wore her hair in a short tapered style that emphasized her small, babyish face and fashionable glasses. Extremely organized and detailed, Honey managed a couple of businesses and her family.

As Honey stood up, she felt as if she had just had an out-of-body experience. She moved slowly and stood against the only chair in the room. She then retired to her bedroom for a pleasant sleep. After two hours of darkness, the lights flickered back on.

Honey dreamed of things that were yet to come. She always had those dreams after entering the presence of God. It was as if she were in another world. In the dreams, she would appear before people crying out for help. The faces were empty—no eyes, ears, or noses. They reached out their hands and called out to her, only to disappear, leaving faceless bodies walking aimlessly in a circle. The dreams would occur daily. She often dreamt of people who she never met but would eventually enter her life—Denise Jones was one of these people. They met at a women's business seminar where Honey was the keynote speaker a few weeks after Honey's vision.

In May of 2003, Honey was rushing to the conference room of the Regency Colony Hotel in Atlanta when she bumped into Denise. It was déjà vu; the bump struck a nerve in Honey.

"Excuse me. Are you Honey Holmes? I mean Mrs. Holmes?"

"Yes, I am. And you are?"

"I'm your biggest fan, Denise Jones!"

"You're my only fan, Denise."

"I'm interested in volunteering with your organization," Denise said. "I want to be as powerful as you are in your seminars. You bring the motivation, the energy, and the power. It's so exciting!"

"I see you really enjoyed my services." Honey looked deep into Denise's eyes, sensing that she knew her, even though they had never met. She wanted to know more about this Denise. However, time didn't permit it. She was rushing to her presentation. Honey provided a number for Denise to schedule coffee and a conversation.

Denise was intrigued by Honey's style and technique; she desperately wanted to be her protégé. A petite, thirty-one-year-old paralegal, Denise was loved and respected by her family and friends. Everyone envied her during and after college—until her friends began to marry. She and one other friend were the only ones still standing as singles in a married world. Always giving and holding the hands of others in their time of need, Denise carried a tremendous amount of emptiness in her life. Finding a man was a soul-searching effort, and she needed to understand why her prayers for a husband had never been answered. Despite having a decent salary and the love of many friends and family, she was lonely and somewhat depressed.

In the middle of June, Denise met with her idol—and she hung on every one of Honey's words. How to start a successful consultant business consumed most of the conversation. Denise's admiration for Honey and her great success grew.

"Why are you so powerful?" Denise asked.

"I'm not exactly *powerful*. As a matter fact, all of my success comes directly from God."

"I know God can do anything. We all know that. But what is the real secret, Honey? You can share it with me. I know God can do anything, but come on. God isn't all that!"

"Denise, do you really believe that statement?" Honey was careful not to say too much about her relationship with God. It was not the time or the place. She was deliberately keeping the conversation light to gain Denise's trust. Honey didn't want to come across as spooky or crazy. Getting people to really understand and enjoy the level of love and success Honey held with God was not easy to explain. She also knew that her character and achievements were of great interest to people who desired success. Explaining God's power and anointing to a traditional Christian can be difficult without God's demonstration of power.

Denise continued to laugh and tried hard to maintain her true thoughts regarding God and faith because she wanted to be a part of Honey's world. In Denise's eyes, business and God didn't mix. This faith thing was a little bit much for a professional person.

"Tell me," Denise said, "exactly how did you become so successful in the consulting business and how can I achieve what you have?"

"You already have everything you need. Just use your God-given talent. Whatever you do—don't try to be me or anybody else."

"I don't want to be you, but I do want to learn from you and use that in my professional walk. You see, Honey, I see nothing wrong with learning from those who have already walked in your shoes."

"Let just say walk in their footsteps—not in their shoes. Their shoes may be too little or too big for those seeking to become something that they were not called to be. Use your own gift to be who God called you to be and don't be a duplicate of someone else."

"But, I don't want to make the same mistakes," Denise said. "I want to avoid any errors to get ahead in this world, and you can help me."

Honey nodded. "That is true, but only you and God know exactly what you are called to do. Now tell me, are you called to do training seminars or what? Do you know what you were put on this earth to do?"

"Of course I do!" Denise exclaimed. "I was put here to make money, live life to the utmost, and enjoy the pleasures of the world!"

"Oh really?" Honey laughed. "Denise, maybe I'll meet with you and let you work on my team as a volunteer. Then you can see exactly what I do. I personally don't know if this is for you, but time will tell."

Denise felt that she was on her way to becoming the consultant and trainer of the year—destined to make millions like Honey. Maybe even more. She always dreamed of being the best. And taking Honey's ideas and making them her own was even better than what Denise had thought it would be. She could not wait to get into Honey's camp, take her ideas, and perfect them.

As they parted, Honey promised to call Denise within a few weeks to brief her on the dates and times for volunteer training. Their next meeting would be designed to embrace Denise and establish a line of trust to bring her into the fullness of God. Honey realized that Denise was connected to her for a particular reason, but the reason had not been revealed to her. The revelation of Denise's connection was a matter of God's timing. Honey had a close relationship with God. Her extraordinary connection with God stemmed from Honey's love for studying and listening to the Word of God since the age of twelve. This continued as she matured into her thirties, including several broken and difficult relationships. Having an alcoholic father, a co-dependent mother, and numerous abusive relationships had led Honey to excessive spending and near bankruptcy when she was single. Learning to love the Lord and her fellow man in the power of the Holy Ghost had helped her overcome the difficulties she had experienced in her life.

Honey would spend large amounts of time studying the Word and fasting, often praying in tongues and asking God for interpretation of the tongues. During her daily routine, she would often talk to God and the Holy Spirit. She loved her prayer time. She also realized she could communicate with God throughout the day without spending hours in prayer. Honey's world was filled with many hours of prayer and reading God's Word because she loved it and she knew without a doubt that God loved her unconditionally. She was fashionable, intelligent, and shared a love for understanding the Bible. Honey's husband, forty-eight-year-old engineer and businessman Howard Holmes, shared her love of God.

Howard was a private and simple person who didn't speak much, but when he did, he was powerful. They were polar opposites. Honey was petite, and Howard was tall and slim. She was extremely talkative, but Howard was more reserved. Friends often referred to them as the epitome of humbleness despite their affluent lifestyle and their level of tremendous giving and business dealings.

Denise spent a lot of quality time with Honey during the spring and summer of 2003. Denise vowed however, never to speak with her again after the strange encounter during her last visit at Honey's home and Honey's inexplicable behavior. After five months, Denise received a letter in the mail. Moments earlier Denise envisioned that summer day in Honey's home when the rocking chair moved with no one in it. As she thought of that moment, she found it hard to believe that the chair could move by itself. Denise's attention was drawn back to the decorative letter with a sweet fragrance of a woman. It was an invitation to Honey's next women's conference in January.

Honey's invitation stirred Denise's interest, but she was also afraid of Honey. Denise had never heard the things that Honey shared about God and her relationship with Him. It seemed foolish, but it touched her spirit. The event at Honey's house had been too much for her, and she decided to separate herself from Honey and the other church members.

The pink and green invitation captivated Denise. The white doves symbolized purity—even though Denise could not quite understand what the card actually meant. The card was skillfully done and gave a clear message that affected Denise. It was a strange feeling, and she could not shake it. Denise placed the letter in her purse and headed to the Hair Lace Salon, the top hair spot in town. The clients preferred to call it The Lace. This was a place where women gathered for fashion hairstyles and the latest buzz concerning women on the move, which Denise considered herself to be.

The Lace had a refreshing, contemporary vogue flare with an artistic flavor, which included engraved carvings, custom blinds, decorative chairs, and coordinating pillows from the prominent designers in the area. With a chic look of pure elegance, the place was truly inviting. The stylists were fashionable and contemporary, resembling models from the runways of Paris. Drinks were often served and those who didn't drink often referred to the salon as the undercover "shot house of the new millennium." The city ordinance and liquor codes left the salon with only one option: to serve only wine and non-alcoholic beverages to customers who desired a different type of spirit in order to lift their spirit and imagination during a few rounds of gossip. The prices were expensive, but the talk was cheap and nasty to the core. Jennie Wilson held the crown for most talkative and most accurate. Spoken as a true orator, Jennie held to her namesake M & M: Motor Mouth. If you wanted to know it, she knew it. People listened to Jennie.

Jennie was six foot three. Her long legs towered over patrons as she added hair extensions. Dressed in three-inch heels, she wore the clothes of a local designer. Her hair and makeup looked as if she was ready for a photo shoot. She was slender with the build of a runway model, and the mouth of a runaway hen. On Saturday, November 1, she told the dangerous and adventurous tale of a local pastor, Larry Bell. Jennie believed that he was living a double life—one as a pastor and the other as a drug lord of a major drug ring. Denise and others listened to every detail of her words.

"Girl, my cousin said that he has been a part of this ring for years. He orders his associate pastors to carry the drugs to missionaries in Mexico and other drug-infested areas, claiming to be working for the Lord. His name is not imprinted on any of the items, but he has a secret system. Not even his family knows of his second life—a life he lived prior to joining the church. He is a true drug lord and gangster," Jennie said as she shook her head.

From a salon chair across from Jennie, one patron asked, "If he is such a gangster, then why are you talking about him? Do you not fear death?"

Another patron yelled, "I know that's right. Don't let anybody come up in here and shoot all of us for listening to you!"

Jennie smiled like a bewitched witch. "They are not going to shoot me. I'm packing and I know people. They may get all of you, but not me. Girl, it's the truth—so help me God. And he is about to tell the congregation tomorrow."

"Tomorrow?" Denise yelled.

"That's right, with the feds standing right behind him. I have never been wrong before. That man, your pastor, is a drug lord. My cousin is the pastor's secretary and she's not going to lie about that. She is a Christian."

"Jennie, you're always right, but this is too much, girl." A shampoo person moved closer and hit her on the arm. "But, girl, you can create some tales. Remember the one about the pastor and the affair you claimed he was having? Uh huh!"

"Yeah, girl! You claimed you even did her hair!" Denise yelled. "It was his sister from D.C.! What's up with that, girl? You ain't no CNN, girl!"

Jennie stopped in the middle of doing a client's hair and said, "I was right, girl. That was not his sister! And he is still, let me be quiet. You people better wake up!"

Denise was placed under the hair dryer and noticed a pair of designer shoes and a matching handbag on the woman next to her. She admired the style and look of the bag and shoes and desired to know the brand. The woman stood up and walked over to Jennie and looked at her. Suddenly, Jennie fell to the floor and the customers started to scream. The woman sat in the chair next Jennie, and without attending to her, crossed her legs. Denise could only see the bottom half of the woman and her back from where she was seated. She could not see her face.

Denise could hear the woman even under the dryer. She spoke with such authority. "Pick her up if you like. She'll be fine," the woman said.

Jennie slowly got up looking dazed by the fall. "What happened? I was talking and suddenly I felt faint and fell to my face! Girl, where is that Honey?"

Denise removed her head from the dryer. *My goodness. It was Honey Holmes who walked past the woman, causing her to hit the floor! Or did she? That woman is so weird!*

Before Honey left, she paid the bill for Denise as God had instructed her to do and walked to her brand-new Mercedes. As she drove into the hills, she recalled God's voice. God had forewarned her that morning that there would be trouble with Pastor Bell and had given Honey direct instructions on what to do regarding the uproar and the exposure of his ministry. She was given specific instructions from God about what to reveal at an appointed time. The presence of God was upon Honey as always, but it was heavier than other times.

Honey had prayed for hours that morning—and while she was driving to the salon. She also prayed in spiritual tongues. When she entered the salon, she was heavy with the presence of God and His anointing. When she entered the salon, she saw the demonic spirits on Jennie. They had little short faces with deep impressions of evil. They were hanging over Jennie's back. Honey realized that those who didn't walk in this level of God would not see or sense the presence of such spirits. Honey also sensed the presence of evil in The Lace—envy, strife, anger, and bitterness. She continued to pray softly in tongues and listen to God's voice while she was under the dryer. When Honey passed Jennie, the evil spirits surrounding her quickly removed themselves and Jennie hit the floor. Honey and her husband had experienced this on numerous occasions.

Many in The Lace didn't understand what had transpired when Jennie fell to the floor, but other Christians in the salon understood that the presence of God was in Honey. The anointing of God had caused Jennie to fall.

Chapter Two

✤ ✤ ✤

"IF IT GETS ANY more crowded," a woman in the pew in front of Denise said, "somebody is going to call the fire marshal! What did the preacher do? Announce that he was giving gold away?"

The way the crowd squeezed in with their children looking their Sunday's worst bothered Denise. They were dressed in their after five and hip hop best. They were even carrying food and chewing gum in their bags. All around Denise, husbands and wives were holding onto each other as if they were protecting their prey from a meat market. Single women were dressed in Saturday night specials, pants and skirts hugging their hips so tightly it seemed as if they were wrestling with their flesh. A casual observer could easily have thought the zoo had mistakenly let out all of the animals and they were gathering for their daily feeding out of instinct. It even seemed as if the feeding frenzy had transformed into a circus where each animal was trying to outperform the other. Denise had never seen such a sorry looking group. They didn't have any presentation or class.

They aren't even trying. I guess my righteous sister would be proud that I'm here this Sunday. What are these people searching for? Are they searching for food for their souls or for their bodies? Maybe they are searching for money, fame, or fortune.

It was the first Sunday of the month at Greater St. James and the people had gathered as they do every first Sunday. Denise didn't think she'd be sitting in the church with them again, but there she was.

It will take hours to get out of this parking lot. This never seems to be a problem for anyone else but me. I guess I shouldn't mind. As always, people will probably notice how well dressed I am and stop to compliment me. At least that'll take the edge off some of this waiting. I would rather be at the mall, but I guess the pews are comfortable enough.

When the service came to a close, Denise grabbed her purse and attempted to push through the crowd.

"I'm glad you came, Auntie Denise," said a charming little girl pulling at Denise's dress.

"Hello, darling," Denise said, picking her up and kissing her on the cheek. "I'm glad I came to see your pretty little face. What a pretty dress for a six-year-old, my darling Katie."

"Thank you, Auntie. Are you coming over to our house for dinner?"

Denise didn't want to lie to her niece. Her ponytails and heart-melting brown eyes placed everyone under the little girl's spell. Telling the truth would hurt her feelings—even if she already understood. Denise didn't want to spend another evening listening to Katie's mom discuss Denise's "ways." It was Sunday, another good day for shopping, and she didn't want to waste it.

While Denise was trying to think up a suitable answer, her sister came up and squeezed Denise's free hand before removing Katie from her arms. "Hello, Faith. How are you?"

Denise was four years younger than her sister, but she looked, acted, and felt as if she was ten years younger. She hadn't spent quality time with Faith since leaving the church when the pastor announced that he had an affair with a young member and refused to step down. This scandal was just one of the allegations surfacing in the community.

Denise assumed that Pastor Larry Bell believed that God had forgiven him and that the congregation should follow the path of forgiveness—even though the mother of his illegitimate child had been kicked out of the church. Pastor Bell was allowed to remain as pastor because there was no board to remove him. He had established sole control of the church after becoming pastor in 2000. Disturbed by all of this drama, Denise, who vowed never to return to that building, was drawn today by rumors that the pastor was going to announce that he was a drug lord and would be assisting federal agents. Denise could not miss such an announcement! The news came straight from the pastor's secretary's cousin; Denise knew that she would not lie. It didn't matter that Denise didn't know the secretary or her cousin. The fact of the matter was that she just wanted to be there to hear the news. Denise hoped that she would not be spotted by her only sister to whom she had adamantly vowed that she would never return to this building.

It wasn't that she was avoiding Faith, but she had no interest in her sister's lectures about forgiveness and not letting a man lead her from gathering with the saints. Denise preferred to call them a bunch of "aints," including her sister. Faith constantly lectured her about being raised in the church and the traditions of her family. Sometimes she wanted to take a bat and hit her sister in the mouth. Faith was relentless about driving home her point.

If Denise could find some way to see Katie and her nephew Gregory—without seeing her sister—she would be in heaven. However, that usually was not possible. There was something about Faith's sweet spirit that caused Denise to distance herself at times. But through the years, she enjoyed the mother image of her sister. Faith always did the right thing. She was always thinking of others and was an active member of the church.

"I said, how are you?"

"I'm okay, Faith."

"I'm glad you came, Denise. Did you enjoy the—"

"Please don't start. I came. Isn't that enough for you?"

"Okay," Faith said. Denise held Katie's hand as they walked toward the parking lot. Nothing else was said about the service—just as Denise had requested.

Even at six, Katie could feel the tension between the two women. She was familiar with it. She smiled bravely and helped them by changing the subject, telling them about a friend she had met in Sunday School. "I know her name is Joy, Auntie Denise, but I don't know her last name. But if you had dinner with us and we got ice cream, that would help me remember."

"Of course it would," Denise said. "After dinner, when you've had your nap and changed clothes, we'll go."

Not wanting to disappoint her niece, Denise unwillingly followed Faith to her house for dinner. *If it were not for that little precious angel, I would be at the River Front Restaurant having brunch, enjoying the sounds of a nice jazz band while awaiting the opening of the mall. What a day this will be—and all for an ice cream cone.*

As Denise drove from the parking lot of the church, she wondered why there was no announcement about his drug connections. The disappointment of not knowing bothered her. She wanted so much for the rumors to be true. Denise looked back towards the steeple of the church. Directly under the beautiful landmark was the known office of the Pastor Bell. Denise wondered what was lingering behind those walls.

Pastor Bell, known as Bell to those closest to him, entered his office after the service and handed an envelope to a police officer. He beamed.

"Johnson, there's more where that came from. You do your job and I'll share the love. If you fail, I cannot promise what the hands of a man will do to those who don't follow. You get my drift, Johnson?"

A man with red hair and light brown skin smiled as he extended his hand. Johnson shook Bell's hand and took the folder that held $30,000. "Yeah, I get your drift, Pastor Bell. By the way, that was a great service."

As Officer Johnson left the room, Bell kissed a young lady who was seated next to him. She was not the first lady.

"Things are really going as planned. I need you to check with the missionaries in Africa. Remember, my dear, only question them about the food donation and not a word more. Needless to say, I'm not a respecter of persons, my love."

She smiled and walked away in her best Sunday dress and hat. Hattie Lewis had a mix of African American and Hispanic heritage. She bore one of the pastor's illegitimate children and was one of his many secrets. She had no shame. Hattie was twenty-three and came from a poor family. She was full figured and had the beautiful, charming look of a humble, sweet lady.

Hattie had been living in the streets until Pastor Bell and his church started saving women from the streets. Some he saved and some he used for his own purpose—but not for the purpose of God.

After dinner with her family, Denise returned to her home. It was late November and Denise watched the setting of the sun from the patio of her townhouse. She enjoyed reflecting on the past week, especially after dinner with her sister. This was a form of relaxation for Denise—something she had learned from her parents.

She particularly liked the view of Stone Mountain and the way it reached toward the sky. The mountains were beautiful during the fall months. There weren't any trees blocking the view of the mountain, which made Denise wonder if the patio had been built strictly for days like these. Her townhouse was only a year old—and it was considered one of the most upscale in the city. She had spent the last nine months decorating it. It was accented with the finest collection of authentic African artwork. She decorated it with custom furniture, matching designer rugs, and lamps that looked as if they had been imported from France. She wasn't finished decorating the townhouse. There was still a lot of work to be done and much shopping to do.

Looking through the patio window, Denise hated to see anything out of place. As she went inside, she repositioned a book. Straightening the book gave her comfort as she moved toward the shower.

She opened a closet filled with a collection of soft, expensive towels to embrace what she thought was a perfect body. The water from the shower cleansed and refreshed her mind. Stepping out of the shower and dressing herself in her favorite pajamas, she quickly cleaned the shower and placed every towel, soap dish, and cleanser in its proper place. Now that things were in order, she needed to focus on the matters at hand. She removed her calculator from her desk drawer and pondered the price of her beloved home. Realizing she had spent too much money on the townhouse, she figured that she needed to get that company bonus soon to complete the rest of her project. Money had never been an issue for her. Things always worked out with her $85,000 salary. She wanted to train and travel with Honey Holmes. She wanted to *be* Honey Holmes. Denise always managed to enjoy the finer things in life—a character trait she inherited from her father.

As the night passed, Denise listened to the cars and people outside; it always made her think about the many people that lived in Atlanta. The bus, the coffee shops, the restaurants, and the smell of bakeries always gave Denise a sense of upward mobility. She placed the calculator down and retired to her bedroom. She was bothered by thoughts of Honey and her conversations about God and the church.

Chapter Three

❋ ❋ ❋

"THAT'S WHAT I'M TALKING about! Hit him! No, he's getting away! Man, what are you doing? This is crazy!" Hilton Johnson yelled. "Man, I wish he had made that touchdown." He held a faded piece of paper in one hand and a remote control in the other.

Hilton had struggled with dialing this number for several days, but knew that he could never forgive himself if he didn't. While watching the game, he recalled talking to Thomas Clayton, his old high school football buddy, about his broken engagement. He distinctly remembered Thomas's demanding behavior toward him and the dating game.

Thomas laughed, shaking his head. "So you're still living in the past and she has moved on into the future. You need to meet someone nice. You know what I mean?"

"What do you mean?" Hilton had asked.

"Well, I know this young lady who was on my old mail route. She is my wife's friend and she moved in this complex, a couple of doors down from you. She would be good company for you—that's what I mean. Her name is Denise Jones. I want you to meet her. I'll ask my wife to see if Denise is seeing anyone"

"I can't do that, Thomas." Looking at Thomas's huge frame, robust arms, and shiny black eyes, Hilton felt as if Thomas was going to tackle him into making this call.

"Yes, you can. I'll tell my wife to get her home number and find out if it's okay. She's nice looking and she's … you know what I mean," Thomas laughed. Thomas called his wife and he gave Hilton the number which he was now holding

Hilton raised his head and focused on the game as the image of the conversation began to fade. He watched television for another forty minutes with the number in his hand. He was a decent, intelligent, driven, successful twenty-seven-year-old banker worried about a phone number. He turned the television off, sat on the edge of the bed, and picked up the phone—only to place it down again. It was 9:30 pm—too late to call.

Hilton came from a background of drugs and alcohol, but he had opted to follow a path of righteousness. Hilton was two years old when his father left his mother. He never really knew him. He had relied heavily on the men from the Boys Club and other community services to raise him.

His mother had not been equipped with the necessary skills to raise five boys in the inner city. The family struggled for everything that they needed to survive and Hilton learned to hold on to whatever he had. In her younger years, she drank a lot, but she was never out of control. Hilton didn't approve of the drinking or the partying. His thoughts often drifted back to his mother and her drunken friends during those early years of his life.

"Hilton, come inside. I have some friends coming over!" Minnie would yell. Short dresses and Afro wigs were her trademark. Her legs were as long as the Empire State Building. Her hazel eyes shined like the sun—the same eyes that she had passed on to her fifth son. Hilton could hear Bobby Womack playing on the stereo in their apartment as his mother held the screen door open, swaying. This was an all-too-familiar sight for inner city children in the seventies.

"Come on, Hilton. I need you to help set up for my friends!" Minnie was always happy on Fridays. These were the days that Hilton could eat whatever she had for her guests. He knew that there would be no time for his mother to yell about eating too much because she would be too involved with her music, men, and liquor. This would leave Hilton to do whatever he pleased at the age of nine.

Hilton rushed into the house, familiar with his task: move the furniture to make room for dancing, drinking, and plenty of loud talking. Moving the furniture reminded Hilton of moving an old worn toy from his toy box. It had been used so many times, but was still good for use. He moved the furniture with pride because he always wanted to please his mother. However, there was one thing that was not pleasing to him: sharing her with some man that may come over that night. He liked the gifts they brought: candy and potato chips only for him. His brothers were too old to partake in such gatherings. They had their own festivities to occupy their time. The screen door opened and his mother's friend held a bag of chips and cookies. Mary was dressed in bright red hot pants and a red and white halter top. Her earrings were big enough for Hilton to jump through. Hilton frowned at the presence of Mary. He knew she would squeeze his cheeks and say, "Minnie, he's so cute. He'll give the girls a run for their money."

Hilton hated anyone touching his cheeks and he could see her coming right for his face. He frowned as she pulled him close with her large hands that sucked the blood out of his cheeks.

"Minnie, I tell you, he's the cutest thing. He'll give some woman a run for her money." Mary laughed while handing Hilton the chips and cookies.

"Put the music on, Minnie. I feel like shaking that thang. Girl, turn it up!"

Hilton took the chips and cookies to his mother's room where the only television was. He hoped the TV would drown out the laughter and music. Before he knew it, the TV was signing off with "The Star-Spangled Banner," a time when television ended at midnight. He could hear his mother and her friends. He wished it was Monday because it would just be the two of them eating bacon and grits.

Hilton's mother and uncle had drunk enough liquor for the entire family during their younger years. Therefore, he had never acquired a taste for drinking. His brothers didn't mind continuing the family tradition of consuming alcohol. Hilton, however, felt like the protector of his mother when he was young because his brothers fell into the arms of drugs and alcohol. He was the only son that she could depend on. Hilton was charismatic, bright, and good-looking. He believed that he could do all things and learned to rely totally on himself. He held close the values he learned. Always longing to forget his poverty-stricken past, he joined the church and renewed his vows to God. Promising never to carry a spirit of poverty, he vowed to save and prepare for the future.

Hilton was still puzzled the next day by the fact that he could not call Denise. He sat at his desk at Bolder Bank with the stained piece of paper. He held it as he walked to the break room for bottled water. By the time he returned, there was a call holding for him.

"Hilton Johnson, how may I help you? Oh hello, Thomas. Why are you calling me at work, brother man? And no, I didn't call Denise Jones."

"Look man I need you to come out to my daughter's recital. Denise will be there; her niece is on the program."

Hilton felt pressured. "What's up? Is this lady desperate? I'm just kidding. She must be cool if she's your friend," he said while staring at Denise's number.

"Come on, man. You'll just take a look."

"I'll be free this Friday. I guess, okay. But don't embarrass me. Where is it? Yeah, I know where your church is. Okay, seven o'clock. Thanks."

After Hilton lowered the phone, he looked at the number and placed it back in his wallet.

I'm going to a church to meet a young lady. It's a dance recital—not a church service. Will she want my money like the rest of them?

Chapter Four

✤ ✤ ✤

As Christmas approached, there was a lot of tension in Faith Smith's home. In spite of her many attempts to pretend nothing was wrong, it was obvious from her husband's behavior that there were problems. His business partner was allegedly taking money, but Chad could not prove it. At forty, he still had a boyish appeal and a smile that was to die for. Although his hair was graying with age, his body was not. He was in excellent shape. He spent a lot of his time volunteering and giving back to the community. He adored his wife and two children. Chad spent a lot of time with his children since Faith was a nurse and worked different shift hours. He had a drinking problem, according to his wife. The drinking and monitoring the household budget were stressful for Faith. She pressured Chad to return to the church to get counseling for his drinking problem. Chad refused to attend, but he supported any event that his children had at the church. This day was no different than any of the other days that Faith had insisted that he seek counseling.

"Why won't you try?"

"If you think I need help, you really got problems. Just focus on your sister, Denise. As a matter of fact, I totally agree with her about not returning to that place you call a church. It's just a building and the people inside need help. Can you tell me how they possibly can help me or Denise? You're having hallucinations and you need help." Laughing, he picked up another glass of beer.

"Just forget it! You're so unreal to the real understanding of God's word! I give up! Are you coming to Katie's recital?"

"Why would I not come?"

"Now, I have to get Denise there. That would make Katie happy."

"Good luck with that," Chad said as he shook his head. "I don't think you should do that unless you can change the location of the recital."

"I know she's angry about what happened, but how long will she hold on to that?" Faith stood up and walked to the kitchen. She wondered how she could reach her stubborn sister.

"You can forgive a man you trusted that admitted to having an affair while he was preaching from the pulpit. He needs to sit his butt down. That is not so easy to forget, Faith. You're crazier than I thought if you think people will forget about that. That will be the day!"

"Chad, we are all human. We have all made mistakes."

"But we repent and we change or make changes. That man is still the same. How can you support that nut?"

"How can I get Denise to Katie's recital?"

"Go ahead and ignore me. Whatever! You never want to hear the truth. Why don't you just get Katie to ask her aunt? Denise can never say no to Katie."

"Great idea! Can you pick up Katie and Gregory from school and take them to Denise's office? I think it will work if Katie personally asks her aunt. I can't imagine Denise saying no to little Katie."

"I guess I can for Katie," Chad said.

At 4:30 pm, Denise had just completed writing a brief. She was about to take the draft to the attorney's office when she noticed the light on her phone extension. She looked at the clock, hoping the receptionist would soon release the line. She wanted to get out of the office early in order to beat the traffic. It was the rule that the receptionist knew the whereabouts of each staff member.

Get off the phone!

The light on the extension went off and the receptionist entered Denise's office. "You have some people here to see you. And there's a call for you on line one."

Denise stood up. "At this time of day, I get a call and visitors? Who is on the phone and who's waiting?"

"It's your family in the lobby and Honey Holmes is holding."

"My family? Is it my sister?"

"No. It's her husband and children." Ellen was familiar with all of family members of staff that had been there for at least two years.

"Tell them I'll be right out after I take this call. I have to give this brief to an attorney."

Ellen held out her hand. "Okay, I'll let them know. Give me the brief and I'll give it to the attorney."

"Thank you, Ellen." Denise picked up the receiver. "This is Denise. How may I help you?"

"You sound as if you wish I had not called you today, but I did. How are you?" Honey said.

"No, that's not true. I'm busy and have family in the lobby. I cannot talk. I—"

"It's okay, Denise. I'll call you later."

"Honey, I wanted to tell you. I—"

It was too late; Honey had released the line. Denise cleared her desk and waited a couple minutes before going to the lobby. She had no idea why her family was there.

When Denise entered the lobby, Katie ran, grabbed her legs, and screamed, "Hi Auntie Denise!"

Chad had a guilty look on his face. Gregory was looking just like his mother. He stood as tall as his father. He was a handsome thirteen-year-old with long legs and naturally curly hair.

Denise smiled and said, "What do I owe this honor to see you all here?"

"Katie had to come here and ask you a question," Chad said.

"You could have called me, sweetie. It wasn't necessary to come all the way down here. Auntie's listening now. What is it?"

"Auntie Denise! Auntie Denise! I wanted to make sure that you didn't forget about my recital on Friday at my church."

Denise chuckled, "I would never forget such a big event. Tell me what time it is again."

Katie shrugged her shoulders and said, "It's at nighttime."

"Katie! I told you it's at seven! You can't remember anything!" Gregory threw his arms up in the air.

"She's only six, Gregory," Chad remarked. "So we'll see you there at seven on Friday, Ms. Denise?"

Holding Katie's hand, Denise smiled, "I wouldn't miss it for the world. Chad, can I speak with you for a moment? The receptionist will watch the children. It will only be for a moment. Please?"

Chad grabbed Katie's hand. "Have a seat beside your brother, Katie, and be good. Gregory, watch your sister. I need to speak with your aunt."

Katie danced to the office music, hitting Gregory. He glared at her. "Be still, Katie! You're so loud."

"I'll only be a step away, so behave. Dad will be right back."

Chad walked back to Denise's office and seated himself. "What's up? I only have a minute."

"I wanted to know if this was a service or just a recital for the kids. I really cannot take that church or that pastor. Did you hear the latest?" Denise asked.

"No! I have not heard anything and I really don't care. I'll go to that event for Katie and that's it for me. My wife is a different story."

"Rumor has it that that man is dealing in drugs and he is a major player!"

Chad smiled. "Now I know you're crazy! That is ridiculous!"

"No, Chad. I have a reliable source! Faith needs to get out of there!"

"Denise, don't be foolish. You know that man is not dealing and your sister will be there until the building burns down. Besides, I agree with you. I'm not going back in there. I believe that the people are the church and not the building. The Bible says not to forsake the fellowship. But you have gone way past the line when you call a pastor a drug dealer."

"Okay! I'll go to the event for Katie—but that's it for me. I'm done."

Chad shook his head. "Whatever, you and your sister are both crazy. Take me back to my kids."

Chad entered the lobby just as Katie and Gregory were becoming restless.

"There's no need to get ugly, Gregory. I'll handle your sister." Chad grabbed Katie's hand and Gregory followed behind them. "Thanks, Denise. We'll talk to you soon."

Denise waved as they walked to the elevator. Denise was trying to fathom how Faith and Chad had used the child to get her back into that church. *This is just too much.*

❖ ❖ ❖

Friday was approaching faster than Denise could imagine. It had been a very long week and she was exhausted. However, a promise was a promise—especially to such a beautiful little girl. Denise assessed her walk-in closet; it was more organized than a medicine cabinet at a local pharmacy: shoes with matching purses, tops, jackets, hats, dresses, and skirts—some with the price tags still on them. Denise pulled out a tailored royal blue dress trimmed in gold. *That is the winning choice.*

As she held the dress and matching shoes, Denise decided she needed a new dress. She headed to Cherries, the top boutique for any occasion. Cherries was conveniently located next to The Lace. Denise was well known at Cherries because she was a frequent shopper. Denise quickly walked to the back of the store and let the best sales representative serve her. The representative quickly loaded some dresses in the fitting room for Denise. She tried a ruby fitted dress and walked out of the dressing room into the lounge. A lady was looking down to see if the shoes matched her dress. Denise asked the lady if she thought the dress looked nice from the back.

The lady said, "It looks great!"

Denise recognized the voice and took a second look. It was Honey Holmes!

"Goodness!" Denise exclaimed. "You know everybody and you are everywhere!"

Honey smiled and said, "I know God—and you."

"You don't know me! And if you did, you would stop following me!"

Honey looked directly into Denise's eyes. "Sweetie, I don't care to follow you or anyone else. I follow God! I needed a dress for an upcoming event and I shop here often."

Denise returned to the dressing room to change. She decided to take the ruby red dress. As she walked out of the dressing room, she noticed Honey speaking to a man. Denise could not hear what they were saying. As she attempted to read their lips, she saw the man's face. It was Pastor Bell!

Denise knew that Honey was the woman who Jennie had spoken about. She was sure that Honey was having the affair with Pastor Bell. Denise knew now that Honey was not as holy as she appeared to be. Denise now had something on Honey and could not wait to share this dirt with her girls!

As Denise approached the counter, the sale representative informed her that Honey had paid her bill. She could bag her items and leave or add anything else she needed to the purchase.

"What? That lady already paid for me to have my hair and nails done! She is crazy and I'll be glad to take her money!"

The sale representative said, "She does this all the time—even for us. She has a genuine, pure heart and loves to give. Don't miss your blessing and stop others from being blessed—others like Honey."

"What does that mean?"

"You are not appreciative."

"Girl, I don't know what you're saying. I love me and I do appreciate whatever she wants to give! I'll take it all—the house, the cars, the money. Whatever!"

"That's the problem. You do you and not others. You need to show the love and allow others to love you. Be a blessing and don't be so selfish."

Denise gathered the bags and added some shoes to Honey's bill.

❖   ❖   ❖

Moments later, Honey ran into the foyer of her home and began crying uncontrollably. When Howard heard Honey weeping, he ran down the stairs and asked, "Honey, why are you crying?"

Honey appeared extremely angry and disappointed. She had seen evil and deception in the eyes of a loved one. She wanted to help the people he was deceiving. "I just spoke with you-know-who. That nut wants me to do a prayer at his church—a prayer that Bell has prepared for me to say on the night of his Christmas recital. He is still up to no good and I can sense his pure evilness. I tried to explain to that man that he has got to get it right. I can see that he is headed for destruction and it's coming soon. He will not listen to me or anyone. He's crazy."

"I must say," Howard said, "you've come a mighty long way. Usually you would be calling him a stupid butthole and going on and on, using words that I cannot repeat. What a difference a day makes with God and prayer. I can't believe it."

"Stop making jokes, Howard! I'm not kidding!"

Honey knew that Bell had forbidden her from returning to his church since she started to walk in the Spirit and attempted to teach it to the congregation. He was angered by her change and didn't want to be associated with her or her husband. Honey believed that God had already completed everything when Jesus went to the cross. It was finished. Jesus left us with the power of the Holy Ghost and our bodies are His temple. Honey and Howard believed that the Holy Spirit reigns in us. That was something that Pastor Bell didn't care to believe. He wanted the people to focus on him and what he sees. Honey's spirit-filled life was not a part of it.

"I'm serious," Honey said. "He grieves me because I don't know exactly what he is doing—but he is doing something and it isn't right!"

"Honey, try to understand that everyone does not want what you have. You have to pray for him and wait on God. God is not a magician. He is God. He gives us free will to seek Him. He offers us his presence and power to obtain the fullness of God. You want it. Bell does not want it—even to the point of death."

"I really cannot understand why he keeps putting himself in these positions and thinks nothing of it. He wants me to pray after the recital on Friday. I really don't want to be a part of anything that he does. But I sense that God is telling me to go, and I'll go. Not as his sister but as a willing vessel for God."

"Now that's the Honey I know. Just listen to God and not yourself or Bell. Pray the prayer that God has given you and not the words of Bell. Remember, Honey, we all have family that needs help, and Lord knows he needs help. Maybe you can say something that will move him into the will of God."

Honey sighed "I have not been to that church in fifteen years. No one knows that he is my brother. Why would he want me to stand before those people and say what I don't believe?"

✦ ✦ ✦

A couple of doors from Denise's townhome, Hilton was dressed in a fashionable black suit, white shirt, and a tie with colors that blended well with his suit. He brushed his hair and walked out onto the patio. Tonight would be the first time that he would attempt to meet someone new since he had broken off his engagement. He hoped she would not be a greedy, money-hungry person without any values. Having already been involved with someone like that once was enough. He could not take another one. Hilton turned on the TV to watch the stock market. What his money was doing was more important than meeting any girl. She could wait. He had spent years compiling the perfect portfolio. Money and finance were things he felt he could control.

Calm yourself. You're just meeting someone, not marrying them.

Hilton turned the TV off and took a final look in the mirror before walking out to his car. As he approached his car, he noticed a young lady in a red dress coming down the stairs. Her beauty distracted him and he hit his knee on the bumper. She noticed him looking so she smiled and waved at him. As he opened the car door, he smiled and waved back. Then he drove off.

Faith called to Chad from the bedroom. "Could you help Katie zip her dress and help Gregory with his tie?" Shutting her eyes, she held her breath waiting for Chad to object. This was the only thing she had asked him to do since she had arrived home. She really didn't have time to dress herself and check on the kids too. It would take her longer to dress than Chad—and she needed time to take care of her personal appearance.

Chad stuck his head around the corner and yelled upstairs, "I'll check on them both!"

Before he could walk away, Faith yelled, "Oh, and don't forget the video camera and Katie's flowers!"

Chad paused and cleared his throat. "No one ever thought it would be this hard with two parents. Faith, what are you doing?"

Faith pushed the makeup powder aside and yelled, "I'm getting dressed. What you think I'm doing?"

"I don't know, Faith! Please come down here and help me with Katie. Also, I need your help finding the video camera and the flowers! Please!" Chad said.

The please in his voice was a get-up-now-please; therefore, Faith stopped getting dressed to help avoid the possibility of an argument. Rushing down the stairs, Faith grabbed Katie and helped her get into her dress. Katie could barely contain herself.

"Hold still, Katie, or you'll rip this costume." Faith glanced at Chad for some support. "Would you please get the video camera?"

Faith was determined to tell Chad what to do—whether he wanted to hear it or not. When she finished dressing Katie and checking the video camera, she ran upstairs to finish getting dressed. Chad had barely finished putting on his tie and checking on Gregory when Faith came downstairs. "Don't worry. I'll get the fresh flowers for Katie. Let's go!" she said.

Chad picked up the camera. "We have at least thirty minutes, Faith. Why are you in a rush?"

"I know, Chad. I want to get there before Denise gets there."

Chad held the camera and whispered, "So do I."

Hilton was excited as he drove into the church parking lot. As he was parking the car, he noticed the neighbor in the red dress getting out of the car in front of him. She was alone. Hilton quickly closed his car door and walked over to her car.

"So what have you been up to? And why are you here?" Hilton said with a smile.

"Excuse me?" she said. "Do I know you?"

She was indeed the same young lady from his complex. She was even more beautiful up close. *Look at those eyes.*

Hilton hesitated. "No, you don't know me. But you saw me when you were coming out of the townhome, remember?"

"Yes. I waved at you."

"Isn't that funny that we would ... I mean ... both you and I are going to the same place?"

She nodded and closed her car door, "Stranger things have happened."

"Will your husband be joining you? I mean are you—"

"Actually, I'm single," she said.

She could tell that he was interested in her, but she would have to check out his pockets before she even considered wasting her time. He could be a penniless, handsome fool coming to church to pick up women.

Hilton looked at her and thought, *What am I doing? I haven't dated anyone in a year. Now I'm meeting someone here and coming on to a lady I just met. God help me, this is a church. What am I doing?*

"Auntie! Auntie you came to see me! You came!" Katie yelled as she ran toward Denise.

"I'll see you inside, Miss ... Miss ..." Hilton said as he held out his hand.

"Come on, Auntie, mom's waiting. Come over here!" Katie pulled Denise toward Faith's car.

"I'll talk with you inside, sir. Just look for me," Denise yelled as she was being pulled away.

Hilton walked toward the church. As he entered, guilt overcame him. *Here I am in the Lord's house hoping to meet one person and trying to pick up another one in the parking lot. I must do better than this!*

"Sir, sir can you hear me?" the usher said while tapping Hilton on the shoulder.

Hilton looked up. "I'm okay. I was just thinking. I think I'll just go into the sanctuary."

The sanctuary was a vision of serenity and the music was so relaxing. The lights were strategically placed to illuminate the plants that had been placed meticulously on the stage.

Hilton sat down and tried to assess his situation. What was happening to him? He needed some answers. If he had any decency, he would walk out of this church right now and forget about the whole thing. As Hilton held his head down, he felt someone else tapping him on the shoulder. He looked up and Thomas was standing next to him.

"You made it," Thomas said.

Hilton stood up and shook his hand. "I don't think this is a good idea. I tried to pick up someone I saw in the parking lot. I saw her coming out of my complex."

"Sit down, man. Please! First, you would not talk to anyone, now you're trying to spread the love. I think you should take it one step at a time. This is a church. You need to just chill. What are you doing?"

Hilton shook his head. "I know. It's not like me to do that. I was just ... I don't know. Pray for me."

Thomas laughed, "You don't need prayer. You need to forget the woman you saw in the parking lot and focus on Denise. You came here for one purpose—so one thing at a time. Since you never called Denise, I mentioned you a couple times to her, but I didn't tell her you'd be here."

Hilton nodded. Thomas was right. *He would not pursue the young woman in the parking lot—that would not be the right thing to do. But what if Denise is a mug? No, Thomas had good taste in women. What am I thinking? I'm only here to be introduced to someone. That's all.*

✤ ✤ ✤

"Hold still, Missy, we have to fix this." Faith struggled with the straps on Katie's costume. "I'm glad you came, Denise," she said.

"When you drive a little girl halfway across town to personally invite me, I can't help but say yes. I was really surprised that you would use your children to get me here. That was pretty sneaky."

"Auntie Denise! Auntie Denise! Please! We're at church!" Gregory said with a frown. Chad gave Faith the same look.

"Oh, baby. I'm so sorry. It's just that I don't approve of the way your mother handles things. I didn't mean to make you upset." Denise rolled her eyes and held out her arms to hug Gregory.

Faith sneered. "Please, Denise. Gregory is all right. Stop your drama and have a seat with the family. I'm taking Katie to the back."

Denise ignored Faith. "Chad, where are you and Gregory sitting? Please put me at the opposite end from where your wife, Mrs. Nuts, is sitting."

Faith didn't acknowledge Denise's statement. As Denise entered the recital hall, she noticed the guy from the parking lot talking to Thomas. *I wonder if that lustful gentleman has a child in the recital. Why else would he be here? I'm here and single as ever, so he could have a relative in the program that is not his child. He's not bad looking. I guess I'll give him a chance. No, I've got to check him out first. Get the 411 from someone before I extend my precious time to him. He could be a loser. Lord knows I don't need another loser to add to my list. Thomas is Kim's husband—he's my connection.*

Denise followed Gregory and Chad to their seats. She stopped when they reached the area where Thomas and the guy were talking.

"Hello, Thomas," Denise said with a smile.

"Hello, Miss Denise. I was hoping you would be here," Thomas hugged her and extended his hand toward Hilton. "This is my friend, Hilton Johnson. I told you about him months ago."

"This is Hilton?"

"You're Denise?" Hilton asked.

They both laughed.

"Thomas, this is the lady from the parking lot."

"That's wild," Thomas said. They all laughed.

"I have to sit with my family. They're waiting. You have my number—give me a call, Hilton. Thomas, tell Kim I said hello. I'll look for her after the show," Denise yelled as she walked to her seat.

Hilton nodded and said, "I'll do just that."

Denise walked toward the front where Chad, Faith, and Gregory were seated. Faith whispered, "This is not a meat market, Denise, or a social gathering."

Faith moved her legs so that Denise could sit down. Denise moved down and ignored Faith. She sat next to Gregory as the lights dimmed for the show. Out the corner of her eye, Denise could see Honey Holmes and her husband. *Why is this lady following me? She really is crazy.*

After the last performance, Honey and Howard stood to the side as an associate pastor acknowledged the dancers and the production crew. The pastor excitedly announced an event that Honey and Howard were giving in January. It was the same event that Denise had received an invitation to attend. To Denise's surprise, the pastor also announced that Honey and Howard would be doing the closing prayer.

Honey took the microphone as Howard stood next to her. She began to thank God for His Son who died on the cross. She thanked him for His death, resurrection, and ascension into heaven and His being seated at the right hand of the Father.

She prayed, "Father, we thank You for this moment in time. We thank You for Your Son who died, rose from the dead, and is seated at Your right hand. Father, we know that You are the King of Kings and Lord of Lords. The Alpha and Omega, the Beginning and the Ending. Lord, we plead the Blood of Jesus over every family member here today, both young and old. We thank You for the Blood of the Lamb and the power of the Holy Ghost who is the anointing power that is working within all of us."

She started to speak in a foreign tongue and went into an unknown language. Suddenly, she stopped speaking. Howard took the microphone and said, "God is not pleased with the state of the church. There is a judgment coming to those who are deceivers of God's people and His Word. Don't be deceived! God will not be mocked!"

The church was silent. Suddenly people started praying in tongues. Others began to fall to the floor. It was as if the presence of God was actually in the church! People were worshiping God. The lady in front of Denise hit the floor. Denise was trying to help her up while others were passing out. People fell on their faces, including Faith and Chad. Denise felt a presence that she could not shake. Honey continued to pray and then she closed the prayer in the name of Jesus.

It was several minutes before people could move from their seats.

Faith ran to the back of the stage to look for Honey—even though she didn't know anything about Honey or her husband. She spotted Honey in a small changing room and began to ask her about her prayer. After a knock at the door, Pastor Bell entered and interrupted Faith and Honey. He asked to speak with Honey in private, but she refused.

"I need a witness if I'm going to speak with you because you don't believe the hour has come for you to repent and turn from your wicked ways," Honey said.

Faith was standing between Honey and the pastor. She didn't understand why Honey was saying such things to him. Honey continued, "Stop selling what you're selling—it's not of God. Call the missionary and bring them home."

"What did you say, young lady? Who do you think you are talking to?" Pastor Bell demanded.

"I'm talking to you, Pastor," Honey said.

"Honey, what in the hell are you talking about? I asked you to pray a simple prayer and you turn the event into a circus! I had people falling all over the place. Now you're making allegations about me and telling me what to do! What exactly is your problem?"

"Pastor, why are you cursing?" Faith asked.

"Sister Faith, I beg you to stay out of this. This is none of your business. This is between Honey and me. I was trying to form a reunion with my family, but you have other plans. This is ridiculous! I should just—"

"Just what?" Honey asked. "You should just do what you always do? Do you mean violence and threats, Pastor Bell? Go ahead, show your true colors."

Faith looked startled. "Wait a minute, you two. Let's calm down. This is not the place or the time to discuss such things."

"You're right, Sister Faith. It is not the time. Honey, I strongly suggest that before you leave, you come by my office to see me." Pastor Bell walked away without saying another word.

Honey turned to Faith, ignoring Pastor Bell. "Now what is your name, Miss?"

"Well my, my name is—"

"It's okay, baby, don't concern yourself with what just happened. That was nothing. God will take care of that—trust me," Honey said.

"Now tell me your name, sister."

"My name is Faith Smith."

"Now that we've got that out of the way, let's talk about what just transpired out there."

Honey was too excited to talk about the power and the anointing of God.

Faith closed her eyes and took a deep breath. "I have heard of speaking in tongues, but Pastor Bell makes fun of it so we don't do that here. I was so surprised that you did. I was also blown away by the power I felt."

Honey said, "I realize that. That was part of the reason for the anger you just witnessed."

"But I thought it was powerful! Good heavens, it was awesome! Why would anyone hate it? The experience was something else!"

"Some pastors don't understand the true anointing and the power of the Holy Ghost. They will not have anything to do with the Holy Spirit's teaching," Honey said, pointing her finger at Faith. "But there will come a time."

There was another knock at the door. Howard was preparing to leave and was looking for his wife. Honey introduced Faith to Howard. Honey and Howard walked Faith down the corridor to the back of the church.

"Mrs. Smith, give me your address and I'll send you an invitation to my event next month."

"That would be great. I'd be delighted to come. I'll bring my sister!"

Honey smiled and said, "That would be wonderful. I'll see you there. Have a good evening."

"Thank you," Faith replied. "Oh my goodness, I've got to go and find my family. It's 9:30."

Honey was not looking forward to the rest of the evening. She knew that she had to confront her brother, the infamous Pastor Bell.

Honey said, "Howard, I meant to tell you that we need to stay a little later to speak with Bell."

"It's late already and I'm not really in the mood for you and Bell together," Howard replied as they moved toward the exit. "If need be, I can go to the car and you can speak with him privately. I'll wait for you, my dear."

They laughed softly as Honey turned toward Bell's office. She hesitated. "You won't leave me here, will you? You'll wait?"

"I guess. You mean leave you with your people? Your family? I'm just kidding. Call me if you need me to come in. I'll be waiting outside."

As Honey walked back down the corridor, she saw a blond man with a military appearance guarding the pastor's door. He looked at Honey and retrieved a cell phone from his suit pocket. He quickly dialed a number while keeping his eyes on her.

"She's here." He told Honey to follow him. His voice had a tone of authority. He was not one to be questioned.

"Of course," Honey responded. She followed him into a large room filled with personal effects of Pastor Bell's family. Honey thought it was unusual how many doors the room had.

Pastor Bell was seated on the couch with a glass of wine in his right hand and a black book on the table beside him. Hattie Lewis—his presumed lover—was next to him. Her appearance was striking but disappointing. It was apparent that she had managed to obtain the heart and soul of Pastor Bell. Given her looks and appeal, it would be easy for any married man to fall prey to her. Hattie was dressed in a red, fitted suit that revealed all that God had given to her full figure. She wore four-inch, high-heeled pumps. She wore the suit well, but she could stand to lose a couple of pounds. Her full breasts held a strand of golden pearls. Her style was unique—but had been paid for by Pastor Bell.

Bell nodded his head and the guard immediately moved toward a door to the right of Pastor Bell. Hattie followed him through the door. Bell smiled. "Thank you, my brother and my sister. This is a private conversation. My sister, thank you for coming. Of course, having lived with you as a child, I knew that you were a woman of your word. And you having walked in what you and Howard call the Spirit, I knew you would come."

"Don't grieve or blaspheme the Spirit of God. You have been warned and your time is nearing, my brother."

"That is an amusing answer, my sister. However, I believe your beliefs are whacked! Get over it, sister! I was raised with you. I know you and your fake husband! Get real and join me in my church. Tonight, I tried to bring family into my ministry. But you came with some spooky … I don't know what you were talking about!"

"I'm talking about walking in God's anointing and power, my dear brother."

Honey was going to warn Bell of what was to come. If she didn't, the blood would be on her hands and the consequence would be fury on both her and Bell. Honey knew he would reject any of her words unless they were in agreement with his. Nevertheless, she decided to say what thus says the Lord.

"We have the same mother but different fathers. Literally, spiritually, and physically, you have become Satan's son and I choose to follow my father, God. Because of your weakness and desire, the exposure is near. Please hear me. I realize that your biological father left you in a running car with a million dollars of drugs as he ran from the police when you were ten. But you cannot follow Satan under the cover of a ministry because you were rejected by your father!"

Pastor Bell smiled and said, "Prior to you coming, I had a glass of wine to calm my nerves so that I would not go there with you. But you had to bring up a past that I had forgotten and you're attempting to make this a counseling session. Baby, I'm a counselor and I know the game. Don't play me!"

Bell was trying not to let his emotions take over so that he could gain her trust. He needed a respected leader on his team. Honey and Howard would bring a different light and fix his negative image. His goal was to move the ministry to her so that he could focus on the business at hand. "I'll have another glass of wine before speaking another word to you." Honey decided that he had gone far beyond disrespect for the House of God by pouring a second glass of wine. "Bell, I know what you're trying to do. You cannot continue to use people for your advantage. You must walk upright in the eyes of God. This is not an emotional response to your drinking of wine in the church—it's a plea to save your life!"

"Honey, I'm in good health. You're crazy. Just be quiet and help me with my ministry. Can you do that as a favor to your big brother and let what is in the past stay in the past? You're really pushing me. You're a woman of God. What does the Bible say? Forgive one another and move on."

"I know that, Bell, but how can two walk if they don't agree? I don't agree with anything you're currently doing in ministry or in your personal life. I know what you're doing Bell, and God is not pleased. Listen to me! I beg you! I must tell you before it's too late. There will come a time when death will strike you like a lightning bolt—you and whoever is following you. There will be an Ananias and Sapphira act upon you and your staff if you don't stop this foolishness. I know you paid Officer Johnson to lie about the drug dealing and I know all about you, Hattie, and Mexico!"

"What in the heck are you talking about? Look, Honey, everyone knows that you came from nothing! And you're trying to tell me about the Bible? I introduced you to the Word of God! I know that in Acts 5:1–10, Ananias and Sapphira lied about their offering to God and were struck dead. What makes you think someone of your background—who is not a licensed pastor and doesn't have a church—can give me a word? I built this church and I have over 20,000 members! You're out of your league!"

Honey noticed the uncertainty in his voice. He stood up and threw his glass against the wall. He rubbed his hand on his forehead. The sound of breaking glass summoned the security guard, but Bell motioned that he was okay. The guard glanced at Honey and left the room.

Honey proceeded as if someone else was speaking through her. "You'll hear my voice echoing in your ear and you will remember these words: Do right in the eyes of God!"

Honey saw Bell's mouth tighten.

"Honey, I need you to leave." He pressed a button on the table next to the couch. Hattie and the security guard entered the room. The guard reached for Honey's arm and walked her back to the church entrance.

"Mrs. Holmes, have a nice evening and be careful," the guard remarked as he locked the door to the church.

The guard returned to his post. It was ten o'clock when he rang the bell. The sound of the bell was unwelcome for Bell and Hattie, but it was an interruption that the guard was accustomed to in the late hours. It took Bell a moment to answer.

"I wanted you to know that I'm back on post, Pastor."

"Great, bring us the usual," Pastor Bell said.

"Yes sir."

Moments later, the bell rang again and the guard was buzzed into the office. He stood and stared for a minute until Bell gave him the okay. The guard removed a pipe and a plastic bag from his pocket. Bell smiled and handed him $1,000.

"Keep the change and keep your mouth shut."

Hattie smiled and took the plastic bag off the counter. She turned to Bell. "Are you ready now?"

The guard watched her every move. There was something strange about her. It was odd for her to be so aggressive in front of him. She smiled and walked toward a door to Bell's right.

Pointing toward a darkened room that led to a bedroom, Bell said, "Leave us, but be on call. You know what to do."

The guard grinned and walked away. The bedroom was beautifully arranged. It was done in dark purple with a touch of gold. It was everything that any adult would want in a bedroom: a large screen TV, remote-controlled lighting, a beautiful fireplace, a bar, and a refrigerator filled with food.

"This is impressive ... pretty impressive, babe," Bell remarked. He stared lustfully at every inch of her body. Hattie had removed everything but what nature had given her. She then lit the pipe and started to smoke it. Bell handed her a glass of wine, removed all of his clothing, and reclined on the king-sized bed. Hattie stood directly over him. He was on his back, smiling. Suddenly she gasped for breath and fell directly on him. Bell could not move and she was not breathing.

Chapter Five

✤ ✤ ✤

THERE WAS A LIGHT snowfall five days before Christmas. The holiday was really in the air in the city. Denise didn't make a sound as she stood in front of the Notebook, a local coffee shop and bookstore that she often visited with friends and co-workers. She was nervous about seeing Hilton again. She was behaving like a schoolgirl on her first date. When he walked up, she noticed him immediately. He was wearing black pants and a white cotton shirt that accentuated his flat stomach and broad shoulders. She smiled at him as he approached.

"Hello, Denise," Hilton said with a smile. "You look great! I'm glad you picked this place—it's nice. This will give us an opportunity to get to know each other."

Denise noticed his perfect smile and his beautiful brown eyes. *My God, this man is so good looking! Why didn't I meet him when Thomas and Kim were trying to set me up? What was I thinking?*

"Would you like to get some coffee?" she asked.

"I'll just have tea. I don't drink coffee."

"I'll take decaffeinated with cream and sugar please." Denise watched him as he walked to the counter. *If he is, as Thomas says, the perfect gentleman, I think I may have a date to the company Christmas party.*

As Hilton walked back to the table with the coffee and tea, Denise noticed that his body appeared to be in perfect shape.

"I got you a small cup of coffee. The large was two dollars. That is really too much for a cup of coffee," Hilton said as he handed her the coffee.

"That's fine, Hilton. Thank you. I see you are cost conscious."

"Every penny counts," Hilton said smiling.

Hilton had a golden rule regarding money. If Denise was going to be interested in him, he wanted to make sure that she understood his financial beliefs. Their hands touched when Denise reached for the coffee. She found herself feeling flush. She wondered if he noticed how fast she had moved her hand back. Denise stood to remove her jacket.

"Here, let me help you," Hilton said. "I don't want you to think that my mama didn't raise me right."

Denise was pleased with his manners as she seated herself after Hilton helped remove her jacket.

Hilton spoke of his childhood and his career. He even confided that he loved to watch the stock market.

"The one thing I don't talk a lot about is my faith. I want people to see by my walk that I love the Lord. I don't want to push it on them. You know what I mean, Denise?"

"I guess I understand. I've been dealing with that same issue. I don't care to discuss it. Do you know what I mean?"

"I guess I should take a hint and change the subject. Let's talk about your hobbies. What do you like to do?"

"I love to read and write, but we can't do that together. What I love to do as a couple or with a friend is go roller skating, walking, and hiking. I love the outdoors."

"There's nothing like the great outdoors. I love it," he said.

By the time Denise had finished her third cup of free coffee, it was eleven o'clock. She needed to leave even though she was enjoying Hilton's company. She felt like a teenager, getting a warm, fuzzy feeling inside when he spoke.

"I'm sorry, Hilton, but it's getting late," Denise said as she stood up.

Hilton assisted her with her jacket and coat. "Where did the time go? I guess I was talking so much. Let me walk you to your car."

As they left the coffee shop, he held his hand on her back and she felt protected from the world. The moon was full over the skyscrapers of Atlanta. When he opened the car door, his lips were very close to hers. She wanted him to kiss her, but as if Hilton had read her thoughts, he whispered, "I don't kiss on the first date."

Denise shivered, trying to control herself. "That's not my style either," she said as she slid into the car.

"Good."

"Good night, Hilton. I enjoyed the time with you."

"I'll call you soon. Good night, Denise."

Denise thought, as she drove away, of how badly she really wanted him and how good he smelled. He was like a refreshing river and she was a desert wanting to be watered.

Denise's phone rang just as she was pulling out of the parking lot.

"Hello girl. It's me, Jennie, your girl. What's up?"

"Girl, I just had the best date, but I'll tell you about that later. I want you to spread this one around the shop. I found out that Pastor Bell is seeing Honey Holmes. I saw it with my own two eyes!"

The voice on the other end of the phone was silent. "Girl, did you hear me? The drug thing was wrong! It was Honey who is sleeping with Pastor Bell! Hello?"

Jennie said, "Girl, if I was you, I would not talk about that lady. There is something strange about her. I cannot put my finger on it. She pays for people's stuff. Sometimes she pays for all of my clients' new hairstyles. You saw me fall down in her presence. I don't mess with that lady. I heard she was a pastor or something."

"Child, that lady is not a pastor! She is just pretending to be something that she is not!"

"Leave that alone. I don't want any part of that, girl. Let me tell you the big juicy scandal that was just on the news. The day after the recital, Pastor Bell was found with Hattie Lewis. She's dead. They were both naked and she was on top of him! The news said that his cleaning staff found him the next morning—and drugs were found too. She overdosed!"

Denise screamed and almost hit the car in front of her. "You're lying! I don't believe it!"

"Yes! It's the truth! He is supposedly in some undisclosed place but will be making a statement."

"I don't get it. I could have sworn the woman was Honey Holmes," Denise said.

"Will you forget about Honey Holmes? This is hot news! Go home and watch the news or just get online. I'll talk with you later. Call me."

News quickly spread about Pastor Bell's unfortunate encounter. Two weeks later, it was still the talk of the town. Denise even heard that the cops questioned Honey, but nothing came of it. Denise spent the remainder of the year with Hilton.

In January, she was making plans to attend a friend's wedding in Florida. She had no doubt that she was going to take the man of her dreams. Showing off your man was the prize reward for every single woman in her social circle. However, the sleeping arrangements concerned her. If she had her way, it would be just the two of them in one room with candles, bubbles, dimmed lights, and nothing on but their birthday suits. She knew that would be out of the question for him—and she didn't want to appear disrespectful or too forward. Denise was startled by the ringing of her cell phone.

"Hello, this is Denise."

"It's me, baby, Hilton. I'm on my way over. I want you to meet my mother and uncle today."

This is big. I'm heading toward the altar. She smiled and said, "That would be great!"

"I know. I wanted you to meet my mom weeks ago, but she works nights and sleeps during the day. Also, I was having so much fun with just you and me. Are you dressed? You know I'm just across the way. I'll be there in, say, five minutes."

"Wait, I need a little more time!"

"Okay, in ten minutes. I'll see you in a few. Bye."

Denise put the phone down. She desperately wanted to text her girls, but there was no time to brag. She ran upstairs to find the perfect outfit. It was cold outside and she needed something striking for this occasion. Hilton said his mother was a simple woman, but what about his uncle? Would he be the one that put her through the test? Denise grabbed a black wool pantsuit, black boots, a purse, and a hat. She was fully dressed when the doorbell rang.

"The party is on," she said as she grabbed her purse and walked downstairs to meet Hilton.

❖ ❖ ❖

"Who's this girl that Hilton is bringing over, Minnie?" Uncle Ed asked.

"Some girl he's been talking about. I don't know," she replied.

Ed Cumming was Hilton's favorite uncle and his fishing partner. He was six feet tall with a boyish face and voice even though he was in his sixties. He spoke like a sailor that had just returned from sea. He said it added some color to his conversation. He was a retired medical technician who worked part-time as a landscaper. Minnie was Ed's only sister in Georgia and they were very close. He was close enough to oversee what the family was doing at all times.

Even at seventy years of age, Minnie looked youthful. She was not as educated as her brother, but she was strong and stubborn. She liked things her way and would often express this to her family. She had a medium stature, but she had a large opinion. Her hair was slightly gray. Because she used public transportation and walked several miles a day, she was in perfect health.

"That boy's going places and he doesn't need a woman tagging along for a free ride!" Ed said, almost shouting, across his sister's kitchen.

"Hilton said that she has a good job. I think she works at a law firm downtown. She's been there for years."

"But what does she look like? He doesn't need an ugly woman in his life. That'll just bring ugly children into the world! We have enough of that in this family. I don't want to see another ugly baby!"

"Afraid they'll look like you, Ed?" Minnie asked laughing.

"No, Minnie, more like you," he said with a smile.

Minnie's two-bedroom house was small and comfortable. It was still decorated as it had been in the sixties. Minnie enjoyed keeping things from the past. The sofa in the living room looked like an old pastel curtain with a paisley print. Above the sofa was a light bulb with a chain. The other rooms were all similar to the living room, but the kitchen had been furnished with more contemporary appliances because of Hilton. He had purchased the appliances when she needed them.

There was a knock at the door and Minnie walked over to answer it.

"I guess that's your future daughter-in-law, the money moocher. Just kidding!"

Minnie ignored him and opened the door for Ed's wife.

Frances Cumming said, "Why are you two staring at me? Let me in. And what was so important that I had to rush over here in the cold?"

Frances walked into the kitchen and took off her coat. Ed depended on Frances to take care of things; she was the support that held him together. She was a strong Christian woman who worked hard as a registered nurse and she did everything she could to keep her house in order. She also made sure that she took care of herself. She dressed in the finest clothes—and her hair and nails were always flawless. She was in her sixties, but looked to be more like a woman in her forties. She had aged gracefully.

"What are you two up to now? Please don't put me in it!" Frances said.

"I ain't up to nothing," Ed said. "It's my sister. She wanted us to come over and meet Hilton's new girlfriend."

"You called me all the way over here for that, Ed?"

"I needed a second opinion. You can't trust my sister's view. She is too … too … she ain't playing with a full deck."

"Who are you talking about, old man? I'm still the oldest and I'll …" Minnie said while raising her hand.

"Look at the both of you, so silly and old. This is foolish. How can you act so silly? Just behave when Hilton comes with his new friend," Frances said.

There was another knock at the door. Minnie walked reluctantly to the door and opened it.

❖ ❖ ❖

Two weeks later, Ed invited Denise to dinner to ask her for assistance with doing his taxes and for some legal advice. Frances and Denise were shopping and attending fashion shows together. They really had a lot in common. Everything was going well with Denise—except for with Hilton's mother. Denise was not very happy that his mother called her Michelle, but Hilton explained that his family was not very good with names. They even called him Milton instead of Hilton. He assured Denise that it was not an indication that his mother didn't care for her, but Denise was not so sure about that.

Spending time with Hilton's family was enjoyable; Uncle Ed and Aunt Frances made her feel welcome. Denise wondered about his brothers and other family members. Hilton's past was no secret. Hilton was Minnie's prized child. He was her greatest reward after four births—and the only child that she could depend on. Minnie hung pictures of him all over the house; he was her greatest trophy.

Hilton and his mother had remained close because he had been the one who assisted   her in her drunken stupors—and during her recovery. He often said that his life had been much different from the lives of the kids he saw on TV.

❖ ❖ ❖

After a month of dating, Denise was feeling troubled by Hilton's sexual behavior. She wanted to discuss it after dinner. The atmosphere was nice and the conversation was going well as they prepared their tea. She was slightly annoyed by the sound of the teapot because it interrupted her thoughts. She walked slowly to the kitchen and removed the pot. Hilton followed her.

"Do you need any help?"

Yes. I need you to come over here, caress me, and kiss me all over. Take me upstairs and relieve me of this desire.

Hilton raised his voice. "Denise! Denise, did you hear me? Can I help you with anything?"

Denise held the teapot. "Sure, the cups are over there. The honey is on the top shelf with the tea bags."

Hilton could not look at her. He knew something was wrong—he was afraid that it was his constant talk about money. She seemed to make a pretty good income—and didn't really have any need for his money—but he just couldn't help himself. Maybe he needed to talk to her about it.

Denise was wondering if she should discuss her strong desire to be intimate with him. She was afraid that he might think that she was crazy and start praying over her, but it was getting really hard to have a conversation with him without thinking about it.

Hilton turned his attention back to the honey and the cups. He removed the top off the honey and placed the tea bags in a cup while Denise poured the hot water over the bags.

"Do you like green tea?" Hilton asked.

"It tastes like grass. I don't like it."

Hilton laughed. "I've never heard that one before. The tea is ready. Be careful—it's hot." They sat across from each other at the kitchen table.

"It tastes like grass, eh? Is that the grass in your yard or the one people smoke?"

"What does a good Christian guy like you know about that?"

"I wasn't always in the church. I know a lot about what goes on outside of the church—and *in* the church for that matter. I was raised in the hood."

"Do you know what a woman needs in her life, Hilton?"

"I know that she needs attention, and she loves affection. She needs a good, caring man that can nurture her and protect her. She needs a good, God-fearing man."

Denise really wanted the relationship to continue, but she wanted an intimate relationship. Her heart knew it—and her body was in agreement. The attraction between them was very strong—and it was becoming more of a problem for her. This was not going to go away overnight. Denise felt that maybe she should not speak of sex to a man who was walking with God—but if God is truth, she must speak her peace.

"That's interesting. Let's move to the living room," Denise said as she carried her tea and two coasters to the living room. The TV was on and she heard an advertisement for the Honey and Howard seminar.

Hilton said, "I know that guy. He introduced me to God."

"What! Do you know his wife?"

"Of course! She is an anointed woman of God and I love her. She is great. Do you know her?"

"Yes! She is weird. Can we not talk about them right now? I need to talk to you about something."

"Let me add one thing. Honey and Howard are not weird; they are anointed and filled with the Holy Ghost. You should attend their upcoming event. They're great."

"I think she's crazy. She has these conferences about building businesses and then the next day she is talking about God and inviting you to some type of session. Then she starts speaking in some foreign language! I really don't like her! Can we please talk about something else?"

Denise was trying to relieve her tension. How many years had she dreamed of meeting this type of man—and falling in love with him? Denise dreamed of enjoying every aspect of Hilton, but that dream had yet to be fulfilled.

What does he want in this relationship? Where are we going with this? Can we take it to the next level?

"Earth to Denise! Where were you?" Hilton placed his tea on the coffee table and took Denise's cup and coaster out her hand. "Oops, I forgot to put my cup on the coaster."

He sensed that Denise was disturbed about something. He wondered if he talked too much about the stock market—or if it was Honey Holmes. Denise appeared to be confused about something; that confusion seemed to be centered on him. Had she decided that she didn't want a relationship with him? Was it all about to end? He had grown so attached to Denise. His thoughts were on her daily.

"Do you have something to say to me, Denise?"

"I have been thinking about us lately, especially you. You are very dear to me and I wanted to talk to you about our relationship. This is kind of silly and I have never had this conversation before. I'm so attracted to you. I see you in my dreams. You are in my thoughts. I think of you when I hear certain songs. I want so desperately to take our relationship to another level. I'm glad that you are respectful of me, but I want to—"

He touched her lips with his finger. "Please don't say anymore. I understand where this is going. Denise, all night I was thinking that you were going to end our relationship because I talked too much about saving money, but if you want to sleep with me, you may want to end the relationship now. It's not that I don't find you attractive. That's why I'm only here a couple of minutes. We spend most of our time with your family or with a crowd. I can't be alone with you for long because it's too tempting. You see, as much as I'm attracted to you, I have a deep relationship with God—and a deeper love of Him. I know that you might find that hard to believe, but it took me a while to get here. It was not easy to get to this point." Hilton stood up and bit on three fingers. "Lord knows it's hard—I mean real hard—when I see you with that wonderful smile and that perfect body. I'm only human. This takes a lot of prayer. I don't want to hurt you, but I'm waiting for my wedding night."

"Hilton, I want you so badly, my body aches! What am I supposed to do? I know about your faith and your beliefs. I worship with you every Sunday. I guess I have to separate from you. I can't take this anymore. I'm accustomed to an active relationship."

"I'm sorry, Denise." He held her chin and looked into her eyes. "My flesh wants you more than you can even imagine. I need to…" He paused, grabbed her, and passionately pulled her close. His heart was pounding. Hilton suddenly turned and ran out of her townhouse. Hilton pushed her desires to a cresting point that was pure agony—and she was sickened by his reluctance to embrace her and her needs. The emptiness of her heart clung to the emptiness of her tears as she fell to the floor and cried for the warmth of a man.

Chapter Six

✿ ✿ ✿

HONEY CONSECRATED HERSELF FOR two weeks prior to her January service, which would focus solely on the teaching of the Holy Spirit. Honey was prostrate in her prayer room. Praise music saturated the room as she entered into a place of love and peace. She felt the presence of the Father and listened quietly as He spoke to her. It was as if she was having an out-of-body experience with God. Her hands were radiating and she felt a warm sensation on her back. Suddenly, as she was praying in her heavenly language of tongues, she saw a vision of her brother.

Pastor Bell was surrounded by trees and brush in an area that appeared untouched by human hands. He was kneeling in a wooded area and was crying out in a drunken rage. His knees were stuck in heavy mud and he slowly clasped his hands to his tear-filled face. Bottles of gin and some unknown drugs were in the mud. He rolled over in the mud like a pig searching for his last meal. His clothing was muddy and torn.

Honey continued to pray in the Spirit. Suddenly, she stopped and was led to leave the room. As she walked the halls of her home, fighting back tears, she stopped near the sofa. Her phone rang. Reluctantly, she answered the call—something she normally would not do during or immediately after prayer. For some reason, she was led to answer the call. As she picked up the receiver, there was a strange but familiar voice on the line.

"Hello, Honey Holmes? Is that you?"

"This is Honey. Who is this?" There was silence on the other end. "Who is this?"

"It's me—Pastor Bell's security guard. Let's just say I'm his right-hand man."

"Let me guess—he is out of control, his wife is not speaking to him, and I'm the only family contact you have. Is that it?"

"Who have you been talking to?"

"I have been talking to God!" she said clearly as tears fell down her face.

"What do you mean? Look, we are in Mexico and he is not supposed to be out of the country while Hattie's death is being investigated! He is out of control and I need help! Tell me who told you what's going on?"

"God told me! What do you want me to do?"

"I need you to come to Mexico to get your brother before he kills himself. We are near the missionary camp built by his church. It's easy to find. As a matter of fact, the location is on the website. When you get here, ask the workers and they will lead you to him. I'm going to leave him in these woods and get the hell out of here. It's all over. It's coming to a head and I don't want any part of it. There is nothing else for me to say. I'm hanging up. Good night." Honey began to pray in tongues and focus her attention on God. She believed that there was no distance between God and a man in need of prayer. She knew that God would intervene and save her brother's life. There was really no need to travel there according to the spirit; she was led only to pray.

The security guard found Bell in a fetal position. He said, "I spoke with your sister. I told her I was leaving you here in these woods! Go ahead! Kill yourself! You're pitiful and you make me sick!"

"I don't care. Leave me! It's all over. Sergeant Johnson told. He told. Why would he do that? I should have killed him! Hattie! Hattie!"

"Man up! I'm out!" The guard turned and walked toward the jeep stopping momentarily to look back at Bell. He opened the door and started the engine. Driving away, he shook his head and vowed never to return to America again.

The guard stopped the car and cried, "Forgive me!" He looked in the rearview mirror. It was too dark to see. "Damn it!" He backed up and drove back toward Bell. He grabbed two flashlights and his gun. He left the jeep running with the lights on and walked toward the wooded area. He heard wailing and a gunshot. He ran through the woods, guided by the two flashlights, the lights from his truck, and the light of the moon.

"Bell! Bell!" he yelled. There was total silence.

Moments later, the guard heard someone say, "I couldn't do it, man. I couldn't do it. I'm such a loser and everybody knows it. What happened? We have been running this game for ten years and made a lot of money. The missionaries had no clue that we were putting drugs in the book covers and shipping them in my private plane. Who told them? That damned Johnson! I knew we could not trust a police sergeant. I should have shot him!" Bell waved the gun aimlessly in the dark. The guard could barely see him or the gun.

"Man, forget him. Let's get out of here."

"You go, my man. I'm going to die right here in Mexico—with all my money and drugs!"

The guard knocked the gun out of Bell's hand and held his own gun to his head. "Now, you listen to me! You're going to do exactly what I say. Get your butt up and move to the jeep! I know you don't want to die. If you did, you would have pulled the trigger!" He grabbed Bell by the shirt and said, "For once, you're going to be a man. Now get up before I blow your head off!"

"I'm up."

"You SOB. I called your freaking sister and told her I was going to leave your butt out here and that I was going to stay in Mexico and start a new life. I didn't care if you lived or died. You made me into a pimp and a drug dealer; you cheated on your wife and killed Hattie! You cheated the church! Man, you're nothing but trash!" The guard was not going back to America, but he wanted to make sure that Bell returned home to face the music. He was determined to get him on that plane.

The guard led Bell through the woods toward the jeep. Bell cried like a baby and continued to share the unknown secrets of his underhanded dealings. As they rode to his private plane, the guard didn't say another word. Once they arrived at the landing strip, the guard told the pilot that Bell was high and needed to get back into the United States as soon as possible.

As the plane left the runway, the guard grabbed his phone. "He'll be there in an hour," he said. The guard released the line, threw the phone out of the window, and drove off—never to be seen again.

The plane landed on the short runway of a private Atlanta airport. Sergeant Johnson walked from an unmarked car toward the plane. Pastor Bell wondered why Johnson had not brought the media or any other cops. He knew that it really was over. His palms were sweaty and his heart was pounding, but there was nothing he could do. As he walked off the plane, he felt anger and pain. He thought about how Johnson had betrayed him and how he should have killed him. He felt like a dead man walking. Bell walked down the stairs and faced his nemesis.

"I knew you would be here to take me in. You're no better than me. How can you take me in?"

Sergeant Johnson stood firmly in front of him. "Man, get over it. I'm an undercover cop. We have been onto you for years. Get ready to pay for your sins, Satan!"

"Perfect. I picked an honest cop." Bell knew how to handle any tight situation and had always managed to get out of them. He decided to remain calm. "Just let me call my attorney before you take me in. And please allow me to call my family … and then there is the church … and my accountant." He was purposely talking fast to confuse Johnson.

Johnson grabbed Bell's arm. "Man, you can call anyone you want once you get to jail. Let me read you your rights and cuff your sorry butt."

"I wouldn't do that if I were you," Bell answered, pushing Johnson to the ground and kicking him. He ran toward the gates, leaving only a fleeing image.

Chapter Seven

❋ ❋ ❋

Hilton and Uncle Ed took a short fishing trip to Florida, but there wasn't any fishing on the first day because it rained. The rain was thick and there was a chilly wind. Hilton and Ed shared a small two-bedroom cabin.

Ed wanted to get Hilton to tell him why he had broken up with Denise. He had secretly promised Denise that he would ask him about the two-week separation. He even promised himself that he would calmly get right to the point. Losing your temper with Hilton always made matters worse. Ed made himself a cup of coffee while Hilton read the newspaper. It didn't surprise him that Hilton was reading the business section. He moved from the kitchen and sat on the sofa next to Hilton.

"Hilton, please don't interrupt me until I finish saying what I have to say."

"It sounds serious, old man. Is Aunt Frances pregnant?"

"Don't count me out. Your aunt is the only one old in this relationship. Just be quiet and listen."

"I'm all ears."

"Where do I begin?" Ed glanced at the kitchen clock. It was getting late. "Let's just get to the point. That young lady—what's her name? You know the one—"

"Oprah Winfrey, I think."

"I don't think that is the one, my son. Unless there is something you haven't told me. I'm talking about Denise. What happened to her? I have not seen her lately."

"How would I know?"

"I thought she was your girl and all. And now, we don't see her."

"Uncle Ed, who is we?"

"Your mom, your Aunt Frances, and your family. Don't get smart with me."

"I'm sorry." Hilton walked to the window. "I just don't want to talk about her, that's all. She is fine ... I guess."

"You guess? Man, a good-looking woman like that and you guess? Didn't I teach you better than that? If I was your age, I would be on it. What has happened to you?"

Hilton remembered his last conversation with Denise, almost forgetting that his uncle was talking.

"Hilton! Boy, can you hear me? What happened between the two of you?"

Hilton wished he knew what to say, but he had no clear answer. He thought about her every day and it made him so unhappy. How could he tell his uncle, a man who believes sex is the answer to all things? He would not understand.

"Let's not talk about this. It's getting late and we have to be up early to catch those big ones."

"Boy, I'm old school and I'll still slap you down. Now sit your butt down and let me tell you something about women, particularly a good woman. Listen to me and keep your mouth shut!"

"Yes sir." Hilton moved toward the sofa and sat next to his uncle. He knew by his tone that he meant business. He wondered why he was so concerned about this girl; she was not the only girl he had ever dated.

"Hilton, I'm going to share something with you and I don't want you to repeat it—not even to your mom. Do you understand me, young man?"

"Yes, I do."

Honey In The Rock

Ed went on to explain the real version of his love affair with Frances. "As you know, we met over thirty years ago in Alabama. Believe it or not, I was the Holy Roller—and yes, your sweet little aunt loved to party. I was preaching and teaching the word and fell in love with your aunt. She could not wait to get me alone. I don't have to say everything. You're grown and understand. I was trying to do the right thing, but she was hot. You can tell by just looking at her. To make a long story short, I didn't do it. Your aunt was on me like white on rice, but I would not break.

"I guess you're wondering what happened to me. Why don't I go to church or believe in any preaching? It's really a long story. Your great grandfather was a pastor and I followed him all the time. We were like peas in a pod. One day I drove by Ms. Annie Mae's house on the way to weekly Bible study and saw his car. I knew it was his car, a white 1954 Ford. No black folks in town had one. My grandmother, moments before I saw his car, had just told me that grandpapa would not be at church that evening. He had to go to the next town to do a funeral and would be back late that night. So when I saw his car at Ms. Annie's, I stopped to see if he was okay and if he needed anything. Sometimes he would stop by members' homes to help them. You can pretty much figure out how this story is going to end. I got out of the car and knocked on the door. There was no answer. So I looked through the window and there was your great-grandpa doing a funeral. Yeah, he was doing his ministering all right, right on top of Ms. Annie with no clothes or Bible. I never went back to any church after that view of your great-grandpapa. I got out in those streets, and I drank plenty of whiskey and good moonshine. I had my pick of women including your aunt, but I never slept with her because I respected her. But the other women were a different story. The streets had me and I was living what I thought was the life.

"I say all that to tell you that Frances turned out to be a good woman. She never gave up on me and my ways. You can see that now. And she is the one still with God; I pretty much gave up. So don't give up on Denise. You just never know. Give it a chance, man."

"Now that was some story. Is it true? And who told you about the problem between Denise and me?"

"Who do you think, fool! Only two people were in the room when the conversation occurred?"

Hilton hesitated. "I don't know what to do!"

"Call her and talk. That is the first step."

"Why can't she call me?"

"You were the one that ran out of the house. Why would she call you if you're running from her?"

"You've got a point there. Maybe I'll call her."

"By the way, the story is true and you do need to call her. I tell you what, even with all the news about Pastor Bell and his dealings, I'll go to church with you if you bring Denise."

Hilton could not believe what he was hearing. "Okay, that will work. But let me pick the time and the place. I want you to go with me to Honey's meeting next week—if that's okay with you."

Hilton had been fishing his uncle for years and now he had the bait to bring him into the kingdom of God.

"Boy, that lady is crazy! And I heard you talk about some of the things she says about walking in the Spirit and praying in tongues. I don't necessarily agree with having to do all of that, but I don't too much agree with anyone who is in the church. Now I believe in God, but I don't really know about the people who claim to represent Him. I guess this one time will not hurt."

"Great!" Hilton said with a smile.

Ed moved toward his bedroom door. "Maybe you can pray about you and Denise at the meeting and see what happens."

Hilton chuckled as he moved toward the room where he would be sleeping. "I already did and I got my answer. Thanks, Uncle Ed. Good night."

❖ ❖ ❖

Denise didn't expect to be so depressed about Hilton. She'd only known him a short time, which was less time than the last nut she had dated. Her depression seemed to be out of sorts—even for Denise. *I don't know why I feel this way.*

Hilton had not called. She'd decided that she was going to bury herself in her work and forget about her problems with Hilton, but it was not working. It had been a great relationship until she had opened her big mouth. Denise remembered that nothing could come between a man and his faith, not even a woman's sexual needs. She had visualized Hilton sitting alone crying out to God to fix the situation. It was silly. Why would he cry out for something that had already been fixed? He was doing the right thing. Maybe *she* needed to cry out and really seek God for herself in order to understand this relationship. Denise thought about Hilton hugging her and walking out of the door; it was as if he was floating on a cloud. She was entertaining an angel from God. How could she sleep with God's angel?

The phone rang and disturbed Denise's thoughts. "This is Denise Jones. How may I help you?"

A familiar voice on the other end of the line responded, "Yes, you can help me and yourself too. Girl, this is your sister. What's going on?"

"I'm working and that's about it. What can I do for you, Faith?"

Faith hesitated. Faith did want something from Denise. She wanted to take her to Honey and Howard's event. A promise was a promise to Faith—and she had promised Honey that she would bring her sister to her event.

"Can't a girl call her sister and check up on her without wanting something?"

"Yeah, but I know you want something. I know you."

Faith didn't want to let Denise know that she was right and avoided making the request until she could ease it into the conversation.

"Look, Faith, I really don't have a lot of time. I'm at work. What's really up? Is it the kids? Is it Chad?"

Faith hated even asking Denise to go to the event. But saving someone for the kingdom was more important than her pride.

"I want you to attend an event with me," Faith said quickly.

"What?" Denise asked. "Can you speak up?"

"I would like for you to attend an event with me and Chad. You can bring Hilton if you like."

"I think you mean join you at that circle of a church with your psycho Pastor Bell."

"No! No! That is not exactly what I had in mind. Let me explain. I need you to attend an event that Honey is having at the Top Civic Center. Remember? She was at the recital three weeks ago."

"Now you have really lost your mind. Are you supporting that crazy lady? No way! I know her personally and she is nuts! I don't think so, my sister. Look, call me later and I'll give you the 411 on that nut!"

"Denise, please don't tell me anymore of your crazy stories. Just let me know if you change your mind. I'll talk with you soon." Faith released the line.

Moments later, Denise's cell phone rang. It was Hilton. He explained that he was returning from a fishing trip with his uncle and asked if she would join him the next week for an event. Before Denise knew what the event was, she committed herself to going. She would have gone anywhere with Hilton. Hilton gave her the date and time and she jotted the date in her calendar. She could not continue the conversation because she had a lot of the work on her desk. Hilton promised to call her later. He purposely avoided talking about their two-week void in communication and Denise was too afraid to bring it up.

Immediately after work, Denise drove down Windsor Way toward The Lace. As she was approaching, she noticed Jennie's car parked in the front of the salon. Denise parked her car and walked leisurely to the front door to see if there were a lot of clients. Usually Wednesday is a busy day for the after-work crowd. Jennie noticed her peeking through the window and motioned for her to come in.

"Hey, girl! Why were you peeking through the window?" Jennie asked.

"I wanted to see who was up in here."

"Why? I'm here that's all you need to know." Jennie walked toward the shampoo bowl to rinse a client's hair. The water ran through the faucet and spilled over on the client's shoulder. "Oh! I'm sorry, baby! I didn't mean to spill that on you. Move up a little."

Denise watched to see who Jennie was shampooing before she spoke. She didn't want everyone in the salon to hear her conversation with Jennie.

"Why are you just standing there, girl? Do you need your hair done or what?"

"No … I want to ask you a question." Denise wanted to talk about Hilton, his short call, his request to attend the event, and even his lack of intimacy. It was inconceivable that Hilton would not explain himself. He was always so detailed and to the point.

"Go ahead. What's the question? Do you need to talk about the color we put in last time? There is a lot of brown in it. I would be more than happy to tone it down for you."

Denise looked straight into Jennie's eyes and whispered, "No. It's private, girl, and I would appreciate a moment of your time."

"You should have said something, girl! You know I always make time for a sister in need." Jennie called her assistant. Jennie rinsed her client's hair and gave her assistant specific instructions. Removing her gloves, she walked toward the back of the salon. "Let's go into the kitchen for some privacy," she said.

An invitation to the private area of the salon was a privilege for clients. The room was truly a mark of money. The kitchen had double ovens, a marble island, and a state-of-the-art refrigerator and cooking accessories. There was nothing left to be desired by any master chef. As they seated themselves in the dining area, Denise said, "Jennie, please don't share this with anyone or I'll just die!"

"Girl, you know I ain't going to tell nobody."

Denise knew that meant as soon as she left the salon, Jennie would be telling every stylist and shampoo person she could find. But at this point, Denise was desperate to talk to anyone—even Jennie, who knew everything about everybody in town. She knew she could not talk to her sister unless she agreed to attend Honey's spooky event.

"Girl, I'm serious. I know how you are. Please, can you keep it to yourself? At least until I get to my car?"

"Am I that bad?"

"Unfortunately you are, Ms. Motor Mouth. I need a listening ear and I need some help with Hilton. I'm begging you!"

Jennie smiled across the table at Denise. She knew that Denise was no different than she was. An intimate gossipy moment was good for Jennie's soul, so she listened attentively to Denise.

"Girl, Hilton called me and mentioned nothing regarding the sex issue or our last conversation. I even talked to his uncle, but I didn't tell Hilton that I spoke with him. I really like him; I just don't understand him. He asked me to attend an event with him next Saturday. He didn't even tell me what the event was."

"It could be a walk in the park or breakfast, I don't know. Denise, why worry? Just enjoy the moment—whatever it is."

"I wonder why he said be ready at 8:30 am outside of my condo—"

"Denise! Denise! What are you looking at, girl? Can you hear me?"

Jennie looked to her left. She realized that Denise was staring at the TV. Honey Holmes was being interviewed by a reporter.

"Turn off the set! She makes me sick!" Denise screamed.

Jennie immediately grabbed the remote and turned the TV up. Honey was explaining the details of her upcoming event. With great passion, Honey explained that the event would deal strictly with the power, anointing, and presence of God and the Holy Spirit. She was expecting great things to occur and asked the reporter to attend. The reporter responded that she may cover the event; she recently had found out that Pastor Bell was Honey's half-brother.

Jennie screamed. "What? See! I told you they were not lovers! I told you months ago when Hattie was found dead that Honey and Pastor Bell were not lovers!"

"Please be quiet. Let me hear this," Denise said.

Jennie and Denise continued to focus on the interview. The reporter, having done all of her research, wanted to talk about Bell— and not Honey's event—since Bell was still missing. The reporter attempted to drill Honey about their connection and if she was harboring a fugitive. Honey answered her eloquently—it was as if someone else was speaking for her. She was calm and to the point. Honey was not concerned about her brother because she was sure that God would handle every aspect of the situation. It was as if it didn't matter that he was running away from the inevitable. Honey's focus was strictly on her expectation of God.

"I know that all is well and that he will learn, sooner or later, that he cannot run from God."

The reporter said, "He is not running from God—it's the police! Why are you wishing for more trouble? Isn't he in enough trouble already?"

Honey beamed as if she were in another world. "Once he surrenders, he will be free. Trouble helps you get there faster because you have no other recourse but to seek God. Bell needs to eliminate all options except God. If he had listened to God, his yoke would have been easy. But now there is a harder road and consequences for him. But God is merciful!"

Denise said, "See! Right there! I told you she was crazy! Why would she hope trouble finds him? He has had enough trouble already! What more can happen to him?"

"Girl, this is too weird. You know what I think? Now it's making sense. See, that's why people come to me and—"

"Jennie, just get to the point!"

"Girl, listen to me. The point is obvious. You're going to Honey's event with your want-to-be man! That's what's up!"

"No! That lady makes me sick! I cannot attend that event—especially now that I know that Pastor Bell is her quack brother!"

"Half-brother," Jennie interrupted.

"Whatever—they are one and the same to me. A brother is a brother. But forget all of that. I have to figure out a way to find out if this is the same event. Help a sister. This may be my last date with Hilton!"

"Hey, you're already on thin ice with this. Remember that your last conversation was short. I wouldn't push it. Denise, just go and be done with it."

Denise picked up a newspaper on the table and saw an ad for Honey and Howard's event. She screamed, "Why is this lady following me? She is everywhere! Look at this!"

"Girl, it will be all right. Just let it ride and go with your man," Jennie said.

"Can you go with me, Jennie?"

"No way! When I'm around Honey Holmes, I get this strange feeling and she makes me faint. There is something about that woman. I don't think that it's bad, but I have a hard enough time being around her when she comes in here to get her hair done."

"Please! I beg you!"

"I can't put my finger on it, but Honey is different—maybe the correct word is odd."

Denise was not getting her way and decided to try another angle with Jennie. Trying to determine what the problem was between her and Hilton meant the world to her and she wanted Jennie to scope out Hilton. Denise needed to know Hilton's hidden secrets and why he would not sleep with her.

"Ms. Thang, I guess you can put your finger on all of the money that my friends are paying you! All it takes is one call to my girls and you are out. We will all be across the street at Mick's Curls!"

"Go ahead! Everybody knows that my work is good—and so do you! I suggest that you don't play with fire!"

"No! You don't want a scandal to spread about you and the owner's husband!"

"Don't threaten me, Denise! You're playing with fire! I would have to call in Bell's people ... I mean *my* people! You get my drift?"

Why would she say Bell's people? If she crossed the line with someone from the streets, it could be dangerous. She needed to be more careful with what she said or she could be in danger. It was rumored that Jennie knew people who knew people.

"Girl, you know that I was just kidding. I'm too scared to do anything like that. Please listen to me. Just be a friend and meet me next Saturday. I don't know if this relationship is over and I'm dying to know what the real deal is with Hilton."

"Don't play me, Ms. Denise, or it will be the last time you play any game! You know that Saturday is my busy day. What am I supposed to do about my clients while I'm trying to scope out the sexual orientation of your man?"

"How much revenue would you lose if you rebooked them for another day?"

"I guess about $500," Jennie said without looking up.

"I'll give you the $500 and you still can make it up. I need you to scope out Hilton. This may be my last time seeing him. You know everyone in this town and I want to know why he won't … you know."

Jennie held her head up. "Yeah, I know. You want to know if I know who his real friends are and not those who appear to be his friends—not the ones he claims—but the ones that he sees in the midnight hour. You can bring him by the salon and I can tell you that. If you just want to give your money away, I'll take it. I realize that I have more connections than you and most of your friends. I know the dark side of this town. I have more information than the six o'clock news! You're right. I want to get paid!"

Jennie and Denise shared the same heart of greed and deception. Jennie would do anything for money and Denise would do anything necessary to get the man of her dreams in bed. She needed to know if he really wanted her—and, if not, what he was hiding. Denise had no option besides Jennie. Jennie was more reliable than the evening news. If there was a problem with Hilton, no one would know better than Jennie. Denise knew her true friends would not spy on a potential boyfriend.

"Jennie, I need to know if he plays the other field. Let me know if anyone in the salon dated him, be it male or female. I need the 411 on him and I know you can do it."

Jennie crossed her long legs and smiled with a look of deception. "You think he is playing you because he won't give it up? Tell me what would happen if the date is not Honey's event. I ain't giving the money back unless I get a percentage or something for my time."

"Jennie, listen girl, you won't be out anything. Since I'm taking a gamble and you're losing out on seeing your clients, I'll give you

$200 at least. Let's see if he looks like he is upset with you being there, then you can leave. You can meet him and scope him out for me. Don't worry about the money. I'll take care of it. You just follow my lead."

"Wait a minute—this sounds kind of crazy. I'll be losing more than $200, and I can't call all of my clients on such short notice. People have lives; you'll have to give me the whole $500 or the deal is off!"

"Hey, calm your nerves. You'll get your money, girl!"

Jennie leaned toward Denise with a chilling expression on her face. "I want my money now—the whole $500! I have to give my clients time to reschedule their appointments. We are professional here. You know we do what we say—if you get my drift. Now go out to the ATM in the lobby and get my money now!"

"Okay! It's all good! I'm going right now. Calm down Jennie!"

Denise was playing with fire and she knew it. She was starting to become fearful of Jennie. There were rumors that some her clients who owed her money ended up missing. Jennie walked over to the cabinet, carefully took a bottle and glass, and returned to the table. Muting the TV and flipping the channel, she saw another story on Bell and Honey. Bell's picture was being shown on every station. Jennie raised her glass toward the television. "I got you, Baby Bell. I got you, baby." Denise looked back at Jennie as she walked toward the lobby. She wondered what Jennie meant by her comments.

Denise felt as if she had been in a conversation with the devil himself. As she approached the ATM, her thoughts wondered. Maybe she should call Thomas. He did introduce her to Hilton. She could ask him if Hilton was gay, but he would not give her the real deal like Jennie would. Was it worth $500 to replace Jennie's clients? What if Jennie was wrong and Hilton was only taking her to a brunch? Denise decided to break the rules of dating and call Hilton.

❖ ❖ ❖

The phone rang a couple of times before Hilton picked up. "What's up, Denise? I just talked to you. Are we still on for Saturday?"

"Yeah, but I just saw an ad for Honey's event. Is that where you're taking me?"

"Does it matter—as long as we see each other? Why do you ask?"

"Hilton, I just wanted to know where we're going."

Denise and Hilton both knew that she was lying. Hilton held the phone for a moment. "Just wear something nice and casual. It's Saturday morning. If that is where I want to take you, will you still go?"

"Of course, I would do that for you."

"Denise, just trust me. Wait and see." Hilton didn't want to share anything with her until the day of the event out of fear that she would not attend. "Look, I'll call you later." He released the line.

Denise reluctantly placed the phone back in her purse and removed the credit card that she had vowed not to use. Entering the code was like selling her soul, but it was too late to turn back from the hell she was partnering with. She removed the $500 from the machine and placed it in her purse. Jennie was still drinking in the kitchen. Denise's lust appeared to be causing her a lot more trouble than she had bargained for. There was no way that Jennie would even give her a receipt—especially if she was drinking.

Denise handed Jennie the money. Jennie smirked as she counted every bill. "I'll find out everything you need to know and I'll be there for you, girl. But you must do something for me."

Denise's heart was beating fast and her hands were sweating. She could hardly speak. "What do you need?"

"Don't worry. I'll tell you when the time is right. I'll see you on Saturday."

Denise walked away, knowing that she had just made a pact with the devil.

Chapter Eight

❈ ❈ ❈

On Monday, Honey's calendar was light. She and Howard owned 150 acres in the Westgate area of Atlanta. They had built several office complexes that housed her primary office and various non-profits. In over ten years of marriage, Howard and Honey had built a very profitable training and marketing business. They modified it according to the voice of God. The non-profit organizations were built to meet the needs of the people whom they served. Homeless shelters for men, women, and children were housed in a professional, caring manner that helped the residents rebuild their lives. Upscale housing for the elderly was being built. The School of the Spirit, which taught on the anointing and power of God, enrolled about five thousand students per year and was growing across the country with online courses. Honey understood and listened closely to the voice of the Lord in her ministry and business. To Honey, her business was God. It was 9:00 am and Honey was briefing her staff on the logistics of the event on Saturday.

"We will be lead totally by the Spirit of the living God," Honey announced to the group of about fifty team leaders who were scheduled to meet with their people and relay the details according to their assignments.

The conference room could hold at least seventy-five people. It was a state-of-the-art center for conferencing with employees domestic and abroad. Honey held nothing back for the spreading and the teaching of God's word. She advised her staff to be mature Christians, staying in daily prayer along with reading the Word of God and worshiping Him. The mission statement of Honey and Howard's company stood front and center on the wall in their lobby. The gold plate on the wall openly announced that they followed the order of God and believed in the full gospel. The mission on the wall read:

> We are here to proclaim Jesus Christ as our Lord and Savior. Our goal is to train and develop disciples to understand, listen, and obey Him through a covenant relationship with the Father, the Son, and the Holy Spirit. Our mission is to help transform people into kings and priests of God through the power and the anointing of God.

The company was privately owned; they had free rein to do as they pleased with the businesses and organization, with the exception of her boards. The boards and all workers were selected personally by Honey and her husband through the anointing of God.

Honey continued to describe the duties of each staff member according to her agenda. She said, "There will be praise and worship songs. The musicians are aware that all music must—and will—glorify God and worship His name. There will be no songs sung that are not biblically based and don't glorify God. Please understand that we are ushering in the presence of God and that this is a very sacred moment. I have no idea how long the worship will last. It is according to God and His will."

A lady in a tailored black and white suit, matching shoes, and a designer handbag with matching custom jewelry raised her hand. She appeared extremely youthful. Her hair was long and as silky black as her skin was.

"Yes! What is your question?" Honey asked.

The young lady stood and said, "Thank you for taking my question. What do we tell the people when they enter the arena?"

"Good question. You welcome them with open arms and let them know that when they enter, they must be silent and join the service of worship. The presence of God will be so strong that by the time the people arrive, they will have no recourse but to fall and worship Him."

The young lady raised her hand again. "Let me continue please, young lady, before you ask another question." Honey wondered who the young lady was. She knew that the young lady's face looked familiar, but she was not one of the regular staff members. Honey stopped in the middle of the session as she heard the Spirit of God say, "She will be used for my glory." She didn't share this with the group; instead, Honey continued with the presentation.

"We will also be there twenty-four hours prior to the people arriving. There will be three shifts of people who will be anointing the room starting at 9:00 am on Friday until 9:00 am on Saturday. Now we all understand that the Holy Spirit is a person, right? As believers, we know and realize that there are several functions of the Holy Spirit."

Honey began to talk about spending time with God and allowing the Spirit of the Lord to lead you out of darkness into the true light of God. She believed, as did her staff, that the Holy Spirit is a counselor, teacher, and that He functions as the operator of the anointing and the power of God. Not only did Honey and her staff believe in the power of the Holy Spirit, they operated in the power and anointing of God, believing that our bodies are the temple of the Holy Spirit. Honey and her staff believed that the Spirit of God can come upon believers through accepting the baptism of the Holy Spirit creating the power and the anointing of God. She explained that the anointing of the Holy Spirit is given to people to demonstrate God's love and power.

The same young lady who spoke earlier said, "I don't understand any of that."

Honey looked at her as if she was speaking from another authority. "In a minute or two, you'll understand exactly what I'm saying. Not only will you understand—you'll surely believe in the power and the anointing of God!"

The young lady looked surprised. "This is my first day. How will I understand?"

"Yes, this is your first day at this organization and you're not in the right meeting according to your understanding, but you're in the right place for God. What is your name?"

"My name is Talitha Lazarus. May I leave? You're scaring me and I don't understand any of this. I came because I volunteered to fold papers in the back. Somehow I walked into the wrong room."

Honey walked toward Talitha with a reassuring smile on her face. "Please don't leave now! We all realize that this session is for mature Christians and you're not accustomed to such talk. Yet, you're here as a testimony to God as you'll see later. I'll be talking to you once this session has ended. Listen to me right now, young lady. This is vital to your understanding."

As Honey walked back to the PowerPoint presentation and clicked on the next slide, a homeless man appeared at the door followed by a staff member.

The staff member looking puzzled said, "I'm so sorry about the interruption, Honey, but you always said that people are first. This is one of the clients from the Sheppard Center for the Homeless and he wanted to thank you. He said he could not wait so he walked right in. His name is Larry."

Honey knew exactly who he was as she turned to face the man. He was wearing a dirty brown raincoat and torn pants that were muddy and stained; his shirt was also filled with holes. He looked as if he was wearing everything he owned. Without any notice, the strange man pulled a gun from his pocket and screamed, "Yes, Honey! I want to thank you from the bottom of my heart!"

He pointed the gun at Honey. She stood there as if he didn't have gun while the staff and volunteers scrambled like ants in an ant farm. The screams were unbearable and there was great panic in the room. There was so much confusion that it was hard to tell who was doing the attacking. People ran out of the room and left the building, trampling each other and leaving what they thought was only the shooter and Honey.

"Yes, Mrs. Honey! It's me—your brother! And this is my thank you for tipping the police and getting Sergeant Johnson to spy on me!"

"Bell, give it up. I did no such thing. You did it to yourself! God gave you a choice and you selected this road. I had nothing to do with it. God will not be deceived by you or anyone else."

Bell pointed the gun directly at Honey's heart. "You're lying! I know you were out to get me!"

Honey stood and looked directly at him without any fear. He fired six shots at Honey. He ran out of the room while she was still standing.

On the floor next to Honey, Talitha was surrounded by a pool of blood. It appeared that in her effort to run from the shooter, she had tripped and hit her head on the marble conference table. Honey kneeled beside her and knew that she needed to lay hands on her and pray, but just as she was about to get started, the police and emergency services entered the room in massive numbers. Guns were pointed and the officers demanded that everyone hit the floor. Once it was determined that the shooter had left the room, they began a search and the emergency unit began to attend to Talitha.

"Please stand back and don't touch her," the emergency service worker said as he checked to see if Talitha was breathing. "She's gone. This lady is dead. Do you know the next of kin? What is her name?"

As the volunteers and staff reentered the room, they stood in shock. Many began to cry, but Honey was calm. "Her name is Talitha Lazarus," she said.

She turned and addressed her staff, "What have I taught you people? Do you believe or don't you believe?"

Honey asked the EMT if she could pray over Talitha before he removed her body. Honey kneeled with most of her staff, praying in their heavenly language.

Then Honey spoke boldly with all power and authority, "Father, I believe that this young lady is too young to go home. It's your will that we have a long life. It's also your will that we raise the dead and lay hands on the sick. I therefore speak the word of God and in faith as I lay my hands on this young lady. I declare and decree that she will live and by your stripes she is healed. She will live and declare the works of the Lord as you sent your word and healed us all, in Jesus' name."

At that moment, Talitha sat up and her wound was sealed, leaving only a slight hole. She was a little disorientated, but she was alive.

"Praise the Lord! To God be the glory!" echoed from the crowd.

The EMT fainted and had to be revived by his fellow workers. The police officers were in shock.

One officer screamed, "Remain calm! Everything is under control!" He tilted his head toward Honey and smiled. "Miss, please remain calm," he said as he walked out of the door. It was Larry Bell.

Honey, for some apparent reason, could not speak to inform the other officers. She knew that it was not the time. Bell slowly disappeared into the crowd.

The news traveled fast about Honey raising the dead woman. Seconds later, the local and national media were all over the campus. The EMTs and the staff appeared on several stations with Talitha and Honey.

Honey continual said on every interview, "To God be the glory. He said that we shall do greater works, especially in these last days, His will be done through the power and the anointing of the Holy Ghost."

❖ ❖ ❖

Bell returned to a plush townhouse and entered through the back security gate. He was still wearing the police uniform. He used a key card to enter the apartment, carefully placing the gun down. He heard the news of Honey and their altercation on the news. The television set was on and it was loud. He knew that he was not alone. He heard the news of Honey raising the young lady from the dead and Honey leaving the scene alive with no injury.

Bell, holding the officer's hat in hand, said, "That witch! She is spoiling my story! She really needs to go!"

A voice was heard from the back room, "I told you, sweetie, not to mess with that woman—even if she is your sister. There is something about her that cannot be explained. It's as if some guardian angel is protecting her or something. You need to focus on us and this minor problem we are having—you!"

Bell angrily replied, "Look baby, that woman is on the news for raising the dead after I tried to kill her! Ain't this a—"

A tall, beautiful woman walked out of a back room and removed $500 from under her breast and put it down next to Bell's gun. "Use this for leaving the country. I took it off some sucker. I'll tell you about that later. In the meantime, give me a big one."

Bell embraced and kissed her like there was no tomorrow. "Jennie, you need to stop sneaking up on me. We need to talk. What is our next move?"

"What do you mean *we*? You have got to get out of here before you're discovered. I cannot take that kind of heat."

"Look Jennie, all of this—the drugs, the ladies—was all your idea. You were the mastermind behind this and I'm taking the heat for you. My wife left me and now I have nothing. No members, no church, no money."

"Your wife was going to leave you anyway after you had that child. You knew it was a matter of time before the feds would catch up with you. Man, you got played. You should not have gotten involved with Hattie and stuck with me."

Bell was totally confused. Could it be that Jennie blew the whistle on him? He thought that he could trust her, but it appeared that she was the one who he should have been trying to kill. "Jennie, are you telling me that you're the one who gave me up to the police? You set me up?"

"What does it matter who did what? You need me to change your identity so you can leave this country and start over, sucker. So what if I was the one? You need to keep your mouth shut and do exactly as I say!"

Bell didn't like being spoken to in such a degrading manner; usually he was the one giving the orders. He had to think fast to get out of this one. If he didn't want to go to prison, he had to play his cards carefully with Jennie. She was harder than any man he had ever dealt with, but he was not going to be played.

❖ ❖ ❖

On Saturday morning at 8:30, Jennie appeared on Denise's doorstep. Denise was afraid to let her in her house.

"I'll be right out!" Denise yelled.

Jennie knew that Denise didn't want her in her home and that she didn't trust her, but that was okay with Jennie. She only wanted to use her for this season and drop her as a client as soon as she had suckered her out of all her money. She needed to get Bell out of the country and start another front for her drugs.

Denise was dressed as if she was going on an evening date at 8:30 in the morning. Her face was fully made up and her boots matched her decorative scarf. It made one wonder exactly what she wore under her coat. It was January and the temperature was twenty degrees. They walked down the stairs in silence.

"Hilton is never late," Denise said.

"That's good because it's cold out here," Jennie responded.

Just as Jennie was beginning to discuss the weather, Hilton drove up with his mother in the front seat and his aunt and uncle in the back. There were too many people for Denise and Jennie to get into the car. Denise was surprised to see the car full of people. She thought she would be surprising Hilton by having Jennie accompany them. Hilton smiled as he got out of the car. "Good morning, Denise. Who is this with you? I'm Hilton!

Jennie held out her hand. "He is a keeper. This man is so fine!" she whispered to Denise. "Girl, you might have to watch me!"

Denise said, "Hilton, I guess we'll follow you. There isn't enough room for the two of us. Jennie was lonely and wanted to do something today. So I hope you don't mind me asking her to come along. Then again, I guess it's okay since you brought along your whole family."

Hilton didn't respond to Denise's remarks, but he did try to accommodate Denise and Jennie. "You can ride with Jennie, you can drive, or you can ride with us if you like."

Jennie said, "No! No! I'll just follow you and let you guys have your moment with family. I'm good. Wait right here while I pull my car around. Where are we going—in case I get lost?"

"Let me give you the directions. Oh, by the way. I have a flyer." Hilton reached in his coat pocket and handed Jennie the directions.

"Okay. This is the place, just as I thought. I know exactly where this is," Jennie said.

Denise walked towards the car and Hilton's mother moved her purse out of the front seat. "Have a seat next to Hilton, Denise. How are you?"

"Thank you, Mrs. Johnson, but you don't have to move your seat. I can just sit in back."

"No problem. Young people need to be together."

Jennie walked to her car, laughing to herself. She opened the door and sat in the driver's seat. Her 2003 BMW pulled up behind Hilton's car as he drove off. She followed them for a couple blocks. Denise noticed that Jennie had turned in the opposite direction—toward the salon. Denise grabbed her phone and desperately dialed Jennie's number.

"Hello, Denise! What now?"

"You're going the wrong way—unless you know of another way!"

Jennie laughed even harder. "No, I'm going the right way to the salon and home to my bed. You don't need me. By the way, thanks for the money!"

"Wait! You promised that you would go with me!"

"Look Denise, grow up! Things change and this has just changed. Tell Hilton he is hot and you better get it right, honey, or I'll jump on that!"

Denise was devastated by the change in Jennie's plan and losing the $500. As she rode in the car, she could not comprehend what had transpired. The conversation was light as they entered the parking lot. The media surrounded the building. Honey had given a special parking pass to Hilton and his guests. The pass was for an entrance at the back of the building and led to a special seating area. Passing the groups of people praying in tongues while the praise music played provided a sense of peace for Denise. This was the same strange feeling from Honey's home. They were seated by smiling ushers and greeters in the front of the platform next to Faith and Chad, which was a total surprise to Denise. Her day was not working as she planned—and now she was seated next to her sister and her husband at an event given by a woman she could not bear to look at.

Denise acknowledged her sister with a smile and a hug before being seated. The service had not started. The music and praise was extremely soothing, sweet to the ear, and moved her inside and out. People raised their hands and lifted their voices to the music as the words to the songs were placed on a screen. The music seemed to go on for hours before Honey and Howard entered the room. An angel appeared and moved about the building. Denise was shocked that she could actually see an image of a person with gigantic wings standing next to the stage. The angel was transparent. Denise could not tell if it was real or if she was hallucinating. She attempted to get Hilton's attention, but he was face down on the floor, speaking in tongues.

Denise got out of her chair and wiped her eyes several times. She could still see the angel. A misty, gray cloud appeared over Honey and Howard. Honey came forward and began to pray in tongues.

Howard said, "There is a move of God across the land and He is not pleased with the action and the move of the church. We must believe in and learn how to operate in the power and anointing of the Holy Spirit. The Holy Spirit is needed just as He was needed by the disciples and Jesus Himself. Please understand that the Holy Spirit entered our human spirit the day we received Christ. We are born of the Spirit of God, according to John 3."

Howard was speaking what the Spirit was saying to Honey. He began to talk about how the Holy Spirit is present at a Christian's water baptism, but there is a separate experience when the Holy Ghost comes upon you. He described the life of Jesus and His disciples, the miracles after the Holy Ghost came upon them, and the anointing they received in the New Testament. He spoke of Jesus being baptized and the Holy Spirit coming upon Him as a dove when he was emerged in water by John the Baptist, according to Luke 3:21. He referenced Luke 4:18 when Jesus said that He is anointed to preach the gospel and that the Spirit of the Lord is upon Him after He was baptized in the Holy Ghost. Thereafter, Jesus performed many miracles. Howard discussed Jesus' disciples and their weak walk with Jesus until the Holy Ghost came upon them. He described them as weak men who argued among themselves regarding who was the greatest and explained why they could not heal certain people until the Holy Ghost came upon them. The disciples received extreme power after they received the power of the Holy Ghost.

Denise held on to his every word, listening intently as he discussed how Peter denied Jesus three times when a young lady questioned his association with Jesus after he was captured by the Roman soldiers. After His resurrection and before his ascension, Jesus told his same disciples in Acts 1:4 not to leave Jerusalem until the Holy Ghost came upon them. Howard emphasized that the disciples followed His instructions to wait for the Holy Ghost to come upon them. Thereafter, the disciples began to perform miracles and the same miracles are being performed in this day and age.

Howard screamed, "Read the word for yourselves! It's all in the Holy Bible. In John 14:12 Jesus says, 'We shall do greater works.' I believe that just like the disciples, we can do greater works in this day and age! Amen."

As Howard raised his hands, thousands of people praised the Lord. "He is worthy to be praised! How great is His name! Wonderful! Counselor! Emmanuel! The Great I Am!"

There were thousands of people giving praise to God. Honey stood on the platform and blew her breath on the crowd. Every person standing fell to the floor! Not a single person was hurt! People were immediately healed of their illnesses!

Honey, with tears in her eyes, took the microphone and said, "In the name of Jesus, be healed in the presence of the living God.

Continue to love Him and study the Word. Renew your mind daily with the Spirit of the Living God. Just fall in love with Him. God said not to have this experience and forget about Him. Spend time with Him and get to know Him. God is not a respecter of persons. You can have the same anointing that my husband and I have. Please, thirst after Him!"

The musicians began to play as the worship leader sang a sweet, moving worship song to God. The people remained on their faces for what appeared to be hours before leaving the building in silence. As Denise, Hilton, and Hilton's family drove home, no one said a word as they listened to the CD of the event. It would take time for them to comprehend what had happened—and for it to settle in their spirits. It was a moment that would remain forever with them in their spirits and their hearts.

Chapter Nine

❀ ❀ ❀

Jennie arrived at her quiet condo at 7:30 pm. There was no Pastor Bell, even after she spoke with him thirty minutes earlier. She wondered if he had taken her advice and contacted the people who could help him get another identity from the underworld. The darkness of the room made her feel uncomfortable. She knew there were many people who wanted to retaliate against her for certain actions she had partaken of in the past. Lights would provide some assurance for Jennie. She hit the light switch on the wall, but nothing came on. She tried a table lamp and still the lights didn't come on. Slowly she moved her hand across the top of the lamp and found that the holder for the bulb was empty. Someone had removed it. Jennie quickly removed her gun from the side pocket of her purse.

"Put that down!" said Bell. He shined a flashlight directly in her face. She gently placed the gun on the desk in front of her.

"Don't try me, Bell! I'm your key! Remember—you need me!"

"I need you like I need a hole in my head, sister. You're nothing but trouble and your time is up!"

"Bell, if you get rid of me, how will that help you and your problems?"

Jennie was not afraid of death. She had been in this situation many times before and had survived. She knew Bell was not a killer. He was a thief and a liar. She could easily talk him down and then kill him. *Who would the police believe? Me, of course! I'm not a common fugitive!*

"Put the gun down, baby, and let's have some fun. You know what I mean."

Bell laughed. "You're a pitiful sight. Those days are over for you and me. You'll not give away such sexy favors where you're going. They will perish with you!"

"Bell, what are you talking about? Calm down, baby! Let's get some light in here before someone gets hurt!

"I'm talking about you, Jennie—your cold heart and the fact that you cannot be trusted. I have got to get rid of you before you hurt somebody else."

He pushed the chair in front of him and stood before Jennie. He had turned off the flashlight. She could not see him, but she could feel his presence. He flashed the light in front of her in order to momentarily blind her.

"You and I are a part of the sickness in this world and we need to be eliminated. You and I are two sick animals. But don't worry, I'm going to take you out of your cage and let you run with the big boys, your friends, the big boys in hell! You see, baby, I know what I need to do. Tonight, you and I'll both find out if there is a heaven or a hell!"

He looked through her and his mind wandered back to his phone conversation with Honey before Jennie's arrival.

Honey had been resting and basking in the Lord after the miraculous event that Bell watched on television. Honey was expecting Bell's call because God had forewarned Honey of his plans. The phone rang at that moment and it was Bell on the line.

"Honey, I'm so sorry for trying to kill you. I honestly thought that you knew of my sins and had me set up. I have since determined that Jennie Wilson turned on me. I'm at her condo right now. Please come over and bring the police."

Bell had known it would take at least thirty minutes for Honey to arrive and at least five minutes for the police to arrive, so he called her while he was hiding in Jennie's garage. He watched Jennie as she drove up the driveway. Bell had already called Jennie to make sure that she was headed home.

He had dialed Honey's number and spoke with her until Jennie got out of the car.

"Honey, I'm a sick man who has done horrible things to my family and my church. I have deceived you and my followers. I'm sorry that I hid money and sold drugs under the name of God. I was led by the greed and power of being a pastor. I had many affairs that resulted in me having a child outside of my marriage. I met and had an affair with Jennie Wilson. She convinced me to start drug trafficking. She was the leader and I was the front man. This is just a short version of the story. I don't have much time before Jennie arrives to explain the details. Please listen to my heart."

Bell began to cry as he explained how he had been fooled by the money and the adoration of the people. He was just like his father who had left him in a stolen car a long time ago. He was still that little boy.

"I don't believe that God is real, but in a moment I'll find out—me and Jennie. Please forgive me. If there is a God, I ask right now that He forgives me for what I'm about to do and that He will show me mercy. Honey, I take that back. I do believe that there is a higher being somewhere, but I have a whole lot of unbelief. This way, I'll know if God is real. It's the only way I can be free and set others free from the hands of an evil witch like Jennie."

Honey silently prayed as she listened to Bell talk. She wanted to be led by the Spirit of the living God for she knew that this was a life-or-death situation. Speaking in the Spirit, she said, "The Lord loves you in spite of your past and He asks that you repent and confess your sin. Confess and forsake your past. Move forward in God. He wants you to go before your church family, ask for forgiveness, and bear the consequences so that you and others can be free."

Bell cried on the other end of the line as he shared that he didn't know if there is a God who loves him. Even if there is a loving God, He would not forgive him for what he had done. Bell cried that he, as his father, deserved to be caged. Better yet, he needed to just end this misery. His life was a mess. There was no turning back and he needed to know if there is really a God. Bell wanted Honey to take over his church. He asked her to raise him from the dead so he could tell the people that God is really a loving God and that there is a heaven and a hell.

Honey explained that she didn't raise anyone from the dead—God did—and she was only a vessel. It was obvious to Honey that he wanted to repent and but he also wanted to die. He didn't know what to do.

"There is no point in killing yourself, Bell. Just ask God to help you and repent for the pain you have caused yourself and others. God will forgive you, but there are consequences for your behavior."

Honey explained that suicide is a sin. If Bell killed himself or others, he would go to hell. Bell gave Honey all the sordid details about Jennie. He let her know that Jennie would be joining him and that he would take care of her.

"Honey, I'm a weak man in a sick world. I want to leave here and take the person who helped me continue all this pain with me. Honey, I want to know if God loves me! Is he a loving God?"

Bell never believed that there was a loving God, but he did believe that there was a place that people go after death. Honey could hear him sniffling and wiping his nose.

"Tell me, Honey, what were those big figures on the camera that looked like angels? And what was that cloudy mist over your head? How did you do that, sis? I have not called you that since high school. I miss those times when we were close, but all of that God stuff made me sick. If there is a loving God, He would not have let my father leave me in the car with all those drugs. I would not have suffered for so long with the pain of abandonment. He would have protected me. How could there be a God if I was suffering? I decided to just go through the motions and use this avenue of being a pastor to make money, become famous, and tell people what they wanted to hear. I knew pain and I knew what they wanted, but you were different. To this day, you believe what I cannot receive—the love of God. How can I, Honey? Don't try to explain. I'll find out soon enough. Tell me how you made those angels and that cloud appear? That was what I saw on the television set, right Honey?"

Honey assured him that the angels were real and God's glory cloud appeared because they were in the true presence of God. Honey and her staff had prayed and prepared the auditorium for days in expectation of the presence of God. She clarified that she and Howard didn't come out of the back until God's anointing filled the room.

"Bell, that presence is only through the anointing of God and the power of the Holy Ghost, which is what I have been trying to tell you for years. You cannot do ministry without it, Bell. Where God's presence is, there is liberty and love. He loves you, Bell. Hear me, Bell? He loves you and will forgive you."

"Honey, that is great, but I don't know if that is true. But in a moment I'll find out. Tell my son and my wife—even though they have left the country. Please assure me that when they do hear what happened to me, you'll tell them that I love them and I'm so sorry. I hope that one day, if there is a heaven, I'll see you again. Take care of God's people and God bless. Please forgive me, but I have a date with destiny. Honey, please listen to me! Honey! I do believe and accept Christ at this moment, but I don't understand His love and His presence. So please accept this as my confession of faith!"

Bell could hear Jennie but had little understanding of what she was trying to say. His thoughts were focused on his last words with Honey and whether or not that confession would make a difference. His mind wandered back to the present and what he needed to do. Time was of the essence. Honey and the police would be there in a matter of minutes.

Jennie screamed, "Bell! Bell! Bell, can you hear me? Take that light out of my face! Move that gun and flashlight out of my face before someone gets hurt and you'll be sorry! Can you hear me or are you smoking that stuff again? I thought you vowed not to touch the stuff after Hattie!"

She felt for the gun that she placed on the table and held it in her hand, waiting for the right moment to kill him.

"You're evil! You need to be destroyed and I'm the one to do it! Jennie, prepare to meet your maker!" Holding the flashlight, he let the light penetrate Jennie's eyes. "This is the last light you'll see for a long time! Do you want to confess your sins before you meet your maker and repent for your evil ways, Jennie?"

"There ain't no God!" Jennie spat. "And that Jesus stuff is a myth that cannot help me! Only I can help myself, man! Now put that damn gun down before I hurt you!"

This was Jennie's opportunity. She could see the silver gun in his right hand. She grabbed Bell's gun and dropped her own. A struggle pursued, but he overpowered her, pushing her into the kitchen. The light switch was hit during the struggle and the darkness disappeared within the sudden light. Jennie could not overtake Bell, so she bit him on the wrist, causing him to drop the gun. Jennie quickly retrieved the gun and pointed it at Bell.

"Don't mess with me! Now you'll pay!"

Bell laughed and slapped the gun out of her hand. They wrestled across the floor as they fought for the gun. Bell had control, but she managed to push him and retrieve it. At that moment, the gun fired and hit Jennie in the chest. She had mistakenly shot herself!

Moments later Bell searched for her gun and attempted to do the unthinkable but could not. He walked into her garage and closed the door. The car had been running during his confrontation with Jennie. The garage was filled the carbon monoxide. Bell prostrated himself in the back of Jennie's priceless Mercedes which she only drove on special occasions, as this was to Bell. He laid there in peace, awaiting the arrival of his sister, Honey, and the angel of death.

Jennie felt her spirit being pulled from her body. She noticed that she was looking down at her physical body. Suddenly Jennie slipped down into a dark hole. There was not any light and the heat was unbearable. Before she knew what happened, Jennie was locked inside a large cage where fire was melting her flesh.

"Where are we?" she screamed. There was no answer—only the lashing pull of her flesh.

"Now you'll see the place you have selected to spend eternity," a voice said.

Worms were eating her flesh as she screamed. Jennie knew of God but only had a form of godliness and had rejected His Son. She selected a life of crime and hatred toward her fellow man. Jennie's life flashed before her eyes and she could see the pain she had selfishly caused others and the many opportunities God had given her to accept Christ.

She screamed, "God, please help me! Take me out this cage! Forgive me, Lord!"

God said, "I'm sorry, but you had every opportunity to ask for forgiveness—now you must suffer the consequences."

Jennie saw several familiar faces, including Bell's.

He was in a cage and screamed, "Lord! I do believe! Forgive me and have mercy on me!"

Worms were eating and pulling on his flesh as he screamed for God. There were flames and the smell was unbearable. The screams were so loud. Bell was tormented not only by the sounds and the smell but also the eating of his flesh. He was truly in hell.

As he cried, the Lord said, "My son, I forgive you. You have asked for repentance but when you return, you must teach my Word. There are many who are depending on you. Your sister is praying for you and her prayers are being heard because she is the righteousness of God."

Bell could see Honey kneeling near his body, praying and asking God to have mercy on him and allow him another chance to live. She reached for his hand as she wept.

She said, "As a priest of your Word and a believer, please allow my brother to live and declare the works of the Lord. I desire that Jennie shall also live, but you have revealed that she does not have a repenting spirit. I pray that her family and friends may come to know you and be at peace with God. I realize that there is nothing that I can do for Jennie. You have revealed that Bell will live and declare the works of the Lord and I thank you for that, my Lord."

Bell's spirit was lifted through a dark tunnel and he could see a shining light. The darkness was enveloped by the bright light, a warm, sweet presence and joyful sounds of praise to God. There were people that he knew truly loved the Lord. His stepmother, Honey's mother, embraced him. There were former members of his church. It was a beautiful place and he wanted to stay.

Bell stood before Jesus. He knew it was Him because he showed him the holes in His hands and on His side.

His presence was so peaceful and beautiful. He spoke with such love and forgiveness. Bell listened to the peaceful voice.

Jesus said, "I forgave you, my son, the day I went to the cross and you accepted me as your Savior. But it's imperative that you have the humble and forgiving spirit of God. You must love as I love. I desire that you have the spirit of righteousness, joy, and peace in our Father, and the desire to feed my sheep. Go back and remember that I'm with you and I'll never leave or forsake you or my people. Please stand for righteousness and understand that my love is immeasurable. If you fall in love with me, you'll see my will as the Father's through the Holy Ghost. Go back, my son. Study the Word and spend time with me as you have this day."

Bell was awoken by people speaking and monitors beeping. He opened his eyes and realized that he was in a hospital bed.

Bell whispered, "Honey, I can clearly say that God is real. I'm so sorry. He has given me another chance. How is Jennie? I didn't kill her. She wrestled with me and the gun went off. Please listen. I'm so sorry. Did she make it?"

"No, Bell, she didn't make it. I'm sorry, but she died. God said because of her unwillingness to repent and her forsaking of his Son Jesus, she must remain in hell."

"Honey, I'm so sorry. Jennie went to hell and I saw her. I was in hell with her. It was horrible and very painful. I'm so sorry that I didn't know how to save her and she died on my watch. Hell is so real and I'm so sorry. But now I know that no matter what happens, from this day forward, He loves me. He said He will be with me so I'm not fearful. He is with me now. He is with me always."

The police entered the room and spoke with the doctors. After they questioned Bell, he was placed under twenty-four-hour guard because he was a fugitive. Bell's demeanor was peaceful and he appeared to be fearless—even if he was going to prison.

Chapter Ten

❖ ❖ ❖

HILTON WAS AWAKENED BY a phone call early Sunday morning.

Uncle Ed said, "Hey, young man, turn on the TV! Pastor Bell has just been captured! This has truly been a weekend for God! I believe now! Boy, what I saw at that event was priceless and it changed my life. I'm going to do my own research and find out more about it. I want to talk to you, and please give me Honey's number and name of her church. Oh, that's okay; she is all over the news about raising Bell and the young lady. We will talk later. Turn on the TV!"

Hilton moved slowly to locate the remote and the phone rang again. "Hello, this is Hilton."

"It's me Hilton, Denise. I'm so sorry. I'm still in shock about yesterday and I wanted to know if you were going to church this morning. I need a better understanding of what happened. Man, that was different. There is something about Honey and Howard. I don't understand any of this, Hilton."

"Denise, that is what is called the anointing of God. Yes, you must get an understanding of the anointing or the seed that was planted will be lost and confusion will set in. The Holy Spirit will not pressure you. He is a gentleman. But we can talk about it on the way to church, and you may ride with me."

Suddenly Denise screamed and there was silence on the line.

"Denise! Denise! Can you hear me?"

"I just heard on the news that Pastor Bell was caught and he is asking Honey and her husband to take over his church! Bell tried to kill himself and Jennie! She's dead! This is crazy! She was Bell's front for his drugs and other dealings! I cannot believe it. Oh my goodness. I cannot take this!"

"Calm down, Denise. Was she really Bell's front? Did you know of her dealing with Bell?

"I must be honest with you, Hilton. I knew she was evil, but she was in the who's who of Atlanta and I wanted her lifestyle. I was aware of her image and style—but not her dealings with Pastor Bell. I noticed that strange things would happen with her when Honey was around. Honey would walk by her and she would fall out! It was as if she could not stand in the presence of Honey. I never understood that, but I did find out how evil Jennie was. One day I'll share that with you. I'm in shock. I cannot believe that she is dead. I wonder if she went to hell. She was so evil. I cannot believe this. It feels like a bad dream. I'm going to need some help. I even thought that she might kill me! I need to get out of here. Please come get me!"

"Denise, are you okay? I'm so sorry about your friend. I pray that she didn't go to hell. Please don't think that. I'll be right over."

"I cannot believe it. It makes me wonder. Just come, please, and I'll go anywhere. Church maybe the perfect place for me right now."

"I'll be right over. I'm so sorry about your friend. Please remain calm."

There was another call as soon as Hilton hung up from Denise.

"Hilton? This is your mom. I want to ride with you to your church and talk about what happened at the service yesterday."

"Mom, what is going on this morning? Everybody is calling and talking about yesterday's event."

"Young man, that was a life-changing experience and it must continue with an understanding, as Honey said. So you're following her, and therefore, I'm following you."

"No, Mom. I'm following God and God only—not Honey or Howard. It's the Holy Spirit operating and moving through Honey and Howard. It's the anointing and not them. They are only vessels making disciples for God and His Kingdom. With that said Mom, I'll pick you up in an hour. We will be attending Bell's church."

Hilton felt that he needed to attend Pastor Bell's church. He picked up Denise and his mother for the morning service. Directly after praise and worship, Honey and Howard entered the pulpit. Hilton knew that his mother and Denise needed more teaching on the Holy Spirit.

Honey said, "I'm here as a representative of God's Kingdom and at the request of my brother, Pastor Bell. By now, you have all heard of the charges against him and the fact that God raised him from the dead on yesterday, but he wanted to speak directly to his people and members of God's Kingdom."

On the video screens in the church, Pastor Bell expressed his sincere sympathy and apologized for the pain he had caused the Body of Christ. He spoke of his connection with drugs and his association with the underworld. Bell realized that this taping would be held against him in the court of law, but after seeing heaven and hell, he wanted to do what was right in God's eyes. Bell admitted to the congregation about his affairs outside of marriage. He humbly stated that he wanted his sister to serve until a leader was selected by the new board. He would not be returning as pastor, but he would be serving as a minister of the Lord from his cell. He thanked them and asked for their forgiveness.

Immediately following Bell's announcement, Honey came back to the pulpit and explained the role that she and Howard would have in the church. Honey and Howard would help in the rebuilding of the church and teaching of God's Word. They would also help the new pastor transition in the church. Honey began to teach the anointing and power of the Holy Ghost, bringing clarity to the people. She spoke of the works of the Holy Spirit, providing biblical support for her teaching. She taught about the guidance of the Holy Spirit and the convictions. She taught from John 16 and the Book of Acts 1:8, which detailed the power of the Holy Ghost

Hilton and his mom listened attentively, but Denise was distracted by the death of Jennie. It was so troubling that she really could not focus on what Honey was saying. Denise wondered if Jennie had given her life to Christ in the end. Did she go to heaven or hell?

Feeling the need to talk to someone, she cried. There was no sexual desire for Hilton as he embraced her. "Why are you crying, Denise? Are you upset about your friend? I'm so sorry."

She whispered, "I was wondering if Jennie was saved and if she went heaven. I would hate to think that she was in hell. What happened to her, Hilton? Her heart was so hard. Could anyone have saved her?"

Hilton held her close and gently brushed away the tears running down her cheeks. He led her to the back of the church lobby. They sat in a vacant room as Hilton held her hand.

"Denise, we don't know what happened between the time the gun was fired and the time she died. We don't know if she repented and gave her life to Christ in her final hour. She is gone now. We can only learn from this situation and move forward in God's Word and trust Him—even in death. The Bible states that nothing can separate us from God, not even death."

Denise looked into Hilton's eyes. "I just spoke with her and now she's gone. I was afraid of her and what she was capable of doing. I tried to use her to scope you out and find out if you were gay because you would not sleep with me. I paid her $500 to spy on you. I'm no better than her and I'm so sorry. I feel so badly. I added to her evil thoughts and behavior. Will God punish me for my lustful desires and evil thoughts?"

"Denise, let that go, ask for forgiveness, and move forward. You must!"

"Excuse me. Denise? I'm sorry to interrupt, but are you okay?" Faith said from the doorway. "I saw Hilton walking you out of the sanctuary. What is wrong?"

Denise ran to her sister and lovingly embraced her for the first time in years. "I'm so sorry if I was mean and evil to you! I don't want to go to hell! Faith, I don't want to go to hell! I'm so sorry Jennie died and I don't know if she was able to change her life. I'm so sorry!" Denise fell to her knees and cried.

❖ ❖ ❖

Denise was finally alone with Hilton after days of work and the leadership classes taught by Honey and Howard. Since Jennie's death, Hilton and Denise had grown closer and become more transparent in their relationship. Denise and Hilton would often visit Bell in prison, encouraging him while he was adjusting.

The leaves began to fall and they still had not made plans for Thanksgiving. Hilton took Denise to the Riverview Jazz Club as a surprise. She didn't know that he was familiar with such an upscale jazz club. It pleased her to be in such a romantic atmosphere. The music was smooth. The excitement of being with Hilton was bubbling inside of her. She had to remember that she was going to take it slowly and see where the relationship was going. There would be no touchy-feely things going on. She must respect his wishes. Then why did he bring her to this romantic environment? This was a small, quaint club for couples who wanted to be alone. The room was filled with twenty tables that seated two people. The floral arrangements were captivating to the eye. The framed work on the walls added romance to the club's simple but elegant look. There was a small, four-person band. Even the view carried Denise to a place where she knew she shouldn't go.

Oh, God. What was this man thinking? We are supposed to be trying to control ourselves. How can I be calm in a place like this? I have to get out of here—or just throw him on the table and have at him! What am I thinking? The Bible says flee from such things. But this could be a good thing because we aren't doing anything! I have to clear my mind and talk to this man like I have some sense. Please! What am I saying? I'm a horny dog who has not had sex in a long time. Let's be real. I need much prayer and fasting. Please God, help me!

"Denise, are you enjoying yourself? Would you like anything to drink?" Hilton asked while picking up the menu. "By the time we order the drinks, the band will … I mean … let's order something to drink, and maybe we can dance or something."

"You don't look like you can dance," Denise teased. "Besides, that would mean, with this music, slow dancing, touching. Hello?"

"I can tell what type of dancing this will be," Hilton said with a smile. "And I know that's why I want to dance. I understand our agreement. We won't get too close. Besides, there are a million people in here."

"Okay. One dance is fine, but no funny stuff. I know you're a weak man."

"Right, I'll go get the drinks. Is sparkling grape juice okay?"

Denise nodded. As Hilton walked away, she looked at his behind and held her hand to her heart. *Lord, have mercy on me. How can I dance with this man without attacking him? This is crazy. I can't do this. He's trying to torment me.*

Hilton returned with the juice. He looked just as nervous as she did. She assumed that it would be difficult for him too. When the moment arrived, he reached out his hand and pulled her up from the table to lead her to the dance floor.

"They are playing our song," he said. At that moment, a young man grabbed the microphone and began to sing "Always and Forever." He placed his hand on her lips, "Don't say one word. Just enjoy the moment."

Denise felt as if she had entered another world; it was as if they were the only two people in the room. Once the music stopped the room was silent. Hilton got down on his knees. "Denise, I know this is kind of sudden, but I have prayed about it. I would like for you to make it forever. I love you. Will you marry me?" He took a diamond ring out of his pocket and placed it on her finger. Denise began to cry.

"Yes! Yes!" Hilton kissed her. They danced around the room and the people in the club began to cheer and clap.

❖ ❖ ❖

Bell was sentenced to ten years in federal prison for fraud and tax evasion. Hattie's death was ruled drug-related and Jennie's dead was ruled an accidental death. Bell's prison ministry and leadership were well known among the prison staff and his fellow inmates. Hilton and Denise's weekly visits proved to be great ministry and support to Bell. His past activities haunted him in prison as there were numerous death threats which he, with God's protection, managed to avoid. In prison, Bell could only depend on God—even if his sister, Hilton, and Denise supported him on the outside. Once the doors closed, life in a cell could not be protected by those on the outside. It was just Bell and God.

Coffee was brewing and the quiet of the house settled in Denise's ears as she rolled over and stepped onto the clean hardwood floors. The touch of the cool, smooth, bronze wood woke her spirit. The smell of the coffee coming from the automatic coffeemaker was right on schedule as it fit into Denise's daily ritual: prayer, coffee, and a shower.

"Hurry, Denise! Denise! Denise! Are you up? Hello, earth to Denise!"

They had grown accustomed to each other's ways after three years of marriage, but they didn't understand the problems Denise was suddenly having with her body. Today—June 21, 2007—she was seeing a specialist to determine what was wrong.

Because of Hilton's love for money, he had done well for himself. Although they lived in a modest home, their bank accounts were not as modest. Denise had to take some days off from work because of her problems.

"Hilton! Please come help me out of the bed! I'm having one of those moments—and I need to use the potty!"

Hilton moved over to Denise to lift her out of the bed. She weighed a mere ninety pounds. She was vanishing little by little. It was heartbreaking to see her look that way, but he still loved her. He wiped the tears away from her eyes, lifted her off the bed, and carried her into the bathroom. "It's all right, Denise. God sent His Word and He's already healed you."

Because her body was so fragile and weak, she could barely move the toilet lever. As she slowly pushed the lever, she was thankful for that small act. She slowly moved into Hilton's arms as he helped her back to their bedroom. Denise was silent for a moment. "I have to tell you something. I know you're probably going to say that this is not the time, but I—"

"What is it, Denise? Are you okay?"

"I'm fine."

Denise held a wrinkled piece of paper.

"Here, this will explain what I'm trying to say. This is from the doctor's office. I should not have kept this to myself. I have known since yesterday."

Hilton took the paper and read it. He looked shocked. "You're … we're … having a baby?"

Denise nodded.

Hilton ran over and hugged her. "I'm so happy! Why would you think it would be a problem?"

"Because of the sickness."

Before Hilton could respond, the phone rang.

"Hello?"

"Hilton? How are you? You sound like you're still sleep at six o'clock in the morning."

Hilton left Denise in the bedroom and walked to the kitchen. "Faith, is that you? Why are you calling so early?"

Hilton walked over to the refrigerator to get some juice and shifted the receiver into a more comfortable position.

"Hello, Faith. She's okay," he said, keeping his voice low. He didn't want Denise to know that he was reporting her medical condition to her sister.

Faith had been concerned about Denise since she became ill. Denise preferred not to concern her but to pray and trust God. Hilton thought that he should keep family members informed in case of an emergency.

"I'm sorry, but I can't talk now. She's getting up. I'll take good notes at the doctor's office."

"I know you will, Hilton. Thanks for keeping me in touch. I don't know what the family would do if she didn't have you."

"They would live their lives like they're doing now, and of course, trust God."

Faith wanted to pray for Denise's visit. By the time Hilton released the line, he had tears in his eyes.

Faith placed the phone down and began to cry.

Her crying woke up Chad. "Baby, are you okay?"

"I'm fine. I was just checking in with Hilton. This truly is a test for the family. I have to call Howard and Honey and share the updates so we can all be in agreement when we pray."

"Sweetie, look at you. We have been studying the Word for a time such as this. We have been taught to be not only hearers but doers of the Word. We will have to trust God and speak healing scriptures over Denise. We must not forget to pray in our heavenly language so that whatever is hindering her deliverance can be revealed."

Chad grabbed her and held her tightly.

"Okay! I know it's all right. Let me go before you choke me. Chad, you're not just telling me the Word, you're walking it. I might add—no drinking! Can't believe it and I'm so thankful. Since Bell went to prison, the church has been healing. His truth has changed our lives as well as others.

"Since Denise's friend died, it scared her to her knees and healed our relationship. You know Denise is not the same person. I cannot believe that she is helping Bell in prison. Chad, we are all walking in a deeper relationship with God and understanding how to operate in the principles of God. It's so rewarding and peaceful, but I wonder if someone will have to die so that Denise can live. I don't know if that is true, but I realize that, like Jesus, we must die to live as Christ died for us. I believe that some parts of Denise must die so that she can live through this attack and serve God. Honey said that Denise had something that she was holding—and maybe it was unforgiveness. But we will not know until we hear from God. Based on our studies and Honey's and Hilton's teaching, we must pray in tongues to find out what is hindering her and speak the Word over it. I know that we wrestle against spirits and principalities and not things of this world."

The door to their bedroom was suddenly kicked in.

Katie screamed, "Mom, Gregory said he's not taking me to school."

Chad grabbed Faith and Katie and started to tickle them both. From there, a pillow fight started. The laughter could be heard all over the house.

❖ ❖ ❖

Dr. Sandra Williams was recommended by Denise's primary care doctor. Her office was filled with Bibles and inspirational pictures. She had praise songs and gospel music playing over the intercom.

A door opened and a nurse called for Denise.

Hilton and Denise followed her to the back to a room where the nurse took Denise's vital signs. Moments later, Dr. Williams entered the room and introduced herself.

She started to question Denise regarding her symptoms: the hair loss, chest pains, joint pains, and shortness of breath. She listened carefully as Denise elaborated on her symptoms. "Denise," Dr. Williams said as she reviewed her notes, "it appears that you have Lupus. Do you know anything about the disease?"

Denise shook her head. "Not really, I've heard about the disease because my brother-in-law's mother died of it."

Dr. Williams said, "Before I can actually diagnose you, I must run some tests on you to confirm it. I'll briefly tell you about the disease. There are three different forms of Lupus. There is Systemic Lupus Erythematosus, which is a chronic disorder of the immune system. There is Discoid Lupus Erythematosus, where the Lupus is confined to the skin. And there is drug-induced Lupus. You appear to be displaying symptoms of Systemic Lupus, but I must do some tests to be sure. My nurse will take your blood and the results will be back in two days. I want you to schedule another appointment so that I can go over the results with you. I'll also give you some information on Lupus. Please be mindful that there is no cure for Lupus, but there are effective treatments with non-steroidal, anti-inflammatory drugs like Ibuprofen, Nasprosyn, Corticosteroids, Prednisone, Medrol, Cortisone, and others. I'll prescribe a low dose of Prednisone for now."

Denise asked, "Do I need to take them now or wait until you determine if I have Lupus?"

Dr. Williams paused as she looked at the chart. "I would rather you take the Prednisone now to begin getting the symptoms under control. There are some side effects to taking the Prednisone but in doses higher than five milligrams. There could be some increase in appetite, weight gain, mood changes, nervousness, and digestion problems. Our office will monitor your medications and do routine blood tests to determine your levels. Although there are always some risks with any medication, there is some good news. It will reduce your symptoms and put you in remission. We will eventually lower your dosage as you improve. Do you or your husband have any more questions?"

"Yes," Denise said, "will I be able to continue to work if I have Lupus? What about my pregnancy?"

Dr. Williams held Denise's hand. "You'll be able to work as long as we get the Lupus under control. But if there is a lot of stress in your life, that may cause the Lupus to flare up. This may prevent you from working. Since you're pregnant, we will monitor you and the medication. This can be a risk for some people—even with the low dose of Prednisone. I recommend that you see your OB-GYN immediately as this places you in the category of being a high-risk pregnancy. But for now, let's just get the Lupus under control. I'm going to give you the number to the Lupus Foundation. They have support groups and educational seminars for Lupus patients and their families. I'm also going to give you a number of a specialist for the baby. I'll have the results for you on Monday. Don't forget to make your follow-up appointment with the receptionist. I've enjoyed talking with you and your husband. I do believe that if this is Lupus, we can get it under control with medication, proper diet, and moderate exercise. I'll let the nurse come in and take your blood. While she's doing that, I'll get the information about Lupus and write the prescription for you. I'll be back."

As they waited on the nurse to come in and draw her blood, Denise hugged Hilton. "It's been a year-long journey for us, Hilton."

"That's okay—as long as we get to the bottom of the problem. And what is the real problem? There are some deep rooted issues and there is something I feel that God wants you to release. Any hidden issues will develop or destroy you and this has been destroying you so far. But you're still here and standing. I really don't know what the root of the Lupus is, but we know what to pray for."

"Yes!"

The nurse entered the room with tubes and a needle in her hand.

"Pull up your sleeves."

After the blood was drawn and the nurse left the room, Dr. Williams returned with the prescription and the material about Lupus. She asked if they could pray together—that was a new one for Denise and Hilton.

Hilton reached for Denise's hand. "Yes, of course. We'll be more than happy to."

Hilton held Denise's hand as Dr. Williams started to pray. She prayed a beautiful prayer for Denise's healing. Denise stood in total silence. She felt that she was going down a hole and knew she had to get better before Hilton realized that she was afraid of the possible death of her and the unborn child.

Chapter Eleven
✤ ✤ ✤

HILTON AND DENISE WERE amazed by the truth and the purity of Bell's words now that he was in prison. They noticed a true change about him and his relationship with God, but Denise wondered if he would convert back to his old ways after his release. Honey would often speak during service about Bell's spiritual and mental progression. The most moving things that Honey spoke of were Bell's admission to doing wrong and his willingness to study the Word and walk right. Honey taught the congregation to repent and become a willing vessel that God can use. Bell was an example of a true willing vessel, but in the back of her mind, she wondered if he would fall after ten years in the pen.

Hilton, Denise, Honey, and Howard were visiting Bell during their weekly service at the penitentiary. Denise refused to use the wheelchair that had been provided by her husband. With the assistance of Hilton and Howard, she walked into the common area to meet Bell. As Bell entered the common area, Honey could tell that Bell wanted to share something with the group. Bell's peace was unreal; his demeanor was amazing to his former members.

Bell's eyes narrowed as he looked into Denise's soul.

"Denise, I heard the visit with your doctor was good and that you're moving forward. I thank God for your healing. Keep walking in it. I want you to know that after three years in here, I'm hearing from God so clearly. He wanted me to tell you that you should let go and be healed. Don't concern yourself with me but with God. When I'm released to the world, I'll be ready. Denise, please understand that I'm freer here than you are out there. Let it go!"

Denise frowned slightly. "How did you know that I—"

"Please, young lady. I know more than you can even fathom because He is speaking and the Spirit knows all things. He wanted me to share that with you. I realize it may be hard to release that hold, but let it go."

Honey smiled. "I believe our visit is complete and God has spoken. The question is whether the servant hears. That, my dear, is yet to be seen."

The conversation continued as Denise gazed into space, pondering the words of Bell. The others laughed and made jokes about Bell's progression and his life-changing events in spite of his prison sentence. He had made peace with God.

The good-byes were sweet and simple for everyone but Denise. Bell's embrace was warm, but Denise could tell that he knew something about her and that troubled her. It was something that she had never shared with others. How could he know so much about people?

Hilton embraced Bell and walked Denise toward the door. He wondered when God would reveal the root of the satanic attack on Denise. Honey mentioned that it is imperative to intercede with understanding and faith while praying in tongues. Intercessors don't have a clear understanding of all the hindrances that can be in a person's life. Only the Spirit knows. There may be hidden issues that are not known to the person we are praying for. They may believe that they have been delivered, but there has not been an actual deliverance, and Satan is still reigning in this area of their life.

Chapter Twelve

✤ ✤ ✤

CANDLES AND CHINA GRACED the table as Hilton and Denise prepared for a celebratory dinner with family and friends. The seating and arrangement needed to be perfect for the guests. This would be a night of change for all of them. Honey and Howard were invited. Faith, Chad, and the kids would be joining them along with Hilton's mother, Uncle Ed, and Aunt Frances. Of course, Hilton could not make a major announcement without Honey and Howard. As they arranged the table, they made sure that everything was in order. It had been three months since Denise's follow-up visit with Dr. Williams and her official diagnosis. Denise was eating well and taking low doses of Prednisone. She was feeling energized. Everyone was excited about her sudden improvement and mobility.

As usual, Uncle Ed was the first to arrive with Aunt Frances and Hilton's mother. Ed's customary double ringing of the doorbell gave notice of their arrival.

"Open this door, young man! Don't keep your elders waiting. I'm going to eat this pie this minute if you don't—"

"Hush old man or I'll be forced to leave you out there! Come on in Mom and Aunt Frances," Hilton laughed as he held the door open for his mother and aunt.

"Don't humor yourself. I'm still old enough to put you across my knee!" Uncle Ed said slightly pushing the door open.

Hilton helped his uncle carry the pie and other items into the house.

"Hilton, I'm glad you came to your senses and helped me, but I could have done it by myself."

"Now you're humoring yourself. I've noticed you taking a number of Honey's and Howard's classes. I thought I actually saw you at church during the early service."

"I guess that would be right if that was any of your business. Besides you're only repeating what your big-mouth aunt or that sister of mine has told you. I'm not ashamed. I have re-dedicated my life and joined the ministry at Bell's old church and I'm loving it! I'm getting a better understanding of the Word. Honey and Howard have helped me find a new love for the Word. To tell you truth, I don't have this urge to cuss you out like I normally would—so that's a great improvement."

"Great, old man. Then I can call you whatever I want?"

"Don't push it, young man. Now what is the major announcement?"

"My wife will do the honor when everyone is here."

"Will Howard and Honey be here? I have some questions for them. Hilton, do you think they would mind?"

"Of course not, old man—as long as you aren't cursing."

Ed raised his hands toward Hilton. "You ain't too young for me to—"

"All right, you two. Don't spoil the night with that foolishness. Come over to the table and help us," Aunt Frances said.

Honey and Howard arrived with several fruit trays and appetizers for an army. Laughter filled the room as Howard admitted that he might have prepared too much food.

"We have one teen who will take care of all the leftovers—my nephew Gregory. And speaking of teens, here's my sister and her family now," Denise said.

"Auntie Denise, we are here and I'm ready to eat," Katie announced as she walked through the door.

Dinner was a time of breaking bread and sharing a common bond among family and friends. The bond was their love for God and keeping Him first in their lives at all times. The conversation moved from lighthearted to serious when Denise made her major announcement. Raising her glass, she asked that everyone join her.

"Can I raise my glass too, Auntie?" Katie asked.

"Yes. Katie and Gregory, pick up your glasses and join us. I'm proud to say that we will be adding another person to the table next year. I'm pregnant!"

"Who is it, Auntie? Who is coming?"

"No, baby, nobody is coming now—but soon. Your mom will explain it to you later, okay?"

Faith embraced Denise. "I'm so happy for you, but I'm also concerned. This is really a big step. Since I'm a nurse, you know that I know that you must use wisdom. I'm here for you."

Ed said, "Just could not hold off could you, young man. You cannot hold yourself. The woman was just beginning to look like somebody. What is done is done! So be it!"

Minnie and Frances couldn't contain themselves. Minnie said, "We are so happy for you two! This is great! I cannot wait for my first grandchild!"

"I am so excited about having a great niece or nephew to spoil! I'm ready to start spoiling the child."

"That's what aunties do!"

Honey hugged Denise and said, "You must trust God and not lean on your own understanding. This child will be a true test of your faith. I pray that—no matter what you are holding onto—you'll let it go and let God. This is not the time to have a form of godliness and deny His power. You must walk with power and authority, my dear, to save you and your child."

"What do you mean? I'm fine and so is my child."

"I mean what God means. But whatever it is—you'll have the authority to win. Just trust God and listen to His voice and not your own."

"I'll try, but I'm confused."

The announcement placed a bit of a damper on the dinner. Suddenly plates and food were being removed. They were concerned about Denise and her health. Everyone assisted in the cleanup and quickly gathered at the door to depart. Chad had not said anything after the announcement, but he felt compelled to give a word of encouragement. "Denise, trust God. And, by all means, keep the faith and never look back."

"Thank you, Chad. I really appreciate your support. Good night."

Uncle Ed walked out with Honey and Howard and bombarded them with questions about the Bible.

"Honey! Howard! Please tell Bell when you go see him tomorrow!" Denise yelled as they were walking down the walkway.

"He already knows! God told him months ago. He will talk with you soon. Love you!" Honey called.

Denise closed the door in silence. She wondered how he knew these things.

❖ ❖ ❖

While Denise slept that night, Honey's words permeated Denise's spirit.

What had Honey meant? Did she know that Denise had struggled for years with the death of her mother and the role that she played in it as a child? She had never forgiven herself for the pain that she had caused her mother. As she slept, the events of her birth replayed in her head. The story had been told to her accidently, but profoundly, by a loving aunt in a moment of bonding.

Jean Eason was the eighth of eleven children and a mother of two. She lived closer to her mother than any other sibling and was there for practically all family gatherings. She was Denise's mother's older sister and often kept the laughter going at family gatherings. During most Christmas dinners, Auntie Jean spoke of the near-death experience of her sister during Denise's birth. The pregnancy had been difficult one. Aunt Jean's sister, who had died at forty-one, was believed to have had Lupus, which was dormant until the birth of Denise.

This was a recurring thought that Denise never shared with anyone. How could Bell or anyone else know that she had been battling with this thought since her mother's sudden death? The family rumor was that Katie's delivery of Denise caused her to have health issues, and Aunt Jean's stories confirmed that she was the main cause of her mother's death. Denise could never forgive herself for causing her mother's death. Why would God allow her to live and not her mother? She had never understood this; it bothered her every time she thought about having children. Would the same curse follow her and would her child kill her as she had killed her own mother? Denise knew that these thoughts were crazy and wanted to stop them, but she could not shake them. She didn't want to have these thoughts in the atmosphere.

Honey and Howard had taught her that whatever she put in the atmosphere would come to pass. They gave example after example of speaking life—not death and negativity. Denise wondered how a child could be responsible for someone's death. Why did she feel so guilty if she had no part in her mother's death? She didn't understand the haunting feelings and she dared not speak about them because she was carrying a child. Denise believed that the sins of the parents fall on the children. She didn't want her family curse to fall on her child. She would just as soon forget about what Honey and Bell had said regarding her letting go. It was gone in her mind but not in her heart.

Aunt Jean said, "Lord, I thought Denise was going to kill my sister." Aunt Jean always ended up apologizing to Denise and explaining that she had meant no harm. She talked constantly about Denise's mom being in labor for twenty-four hours and her escalated blood pressure. Denise never thought that she might be bothered by the talk of the near-death experience, but she was deeply hurt by the conversation.

Aunt Jean said, "It was a warm spring day in March and your mom was in so much pain all during this pregnancy. I had never seen anything like it before. Back in those days in Alabama, we didn't have any doctors and we delivered the babies ourselves. But your mom had a fancy doctor! You see, your daddy and your uncle took you older children to your aunt's house to look after Faith and your other brothers. Your dad and Charles came back to the hospital. Your mama was having labor pains something awful and she was as big as a pig about to be slaughtered. I know because I have seen my daddy kill many pigs! Don't think I can't talk any better than this, I'm just trying to tell you the way it was. I have all kinds of education and I know when to talk, but this right here is just us and family and I can be free. Getting back to the story of how this little thang almost killed my sister; she ain't never been the same since that day and she finally went on home. Give me some water, baby! Don't just sit there looking at me like you don't have good sense!"

Aunt Jean would interrupt the story and point to one of the children in the room. They all knew that one of them had to move quickly and get the water or all hell would break loose. Faith would always bring her the water because she enjoyed helping others. Aunt Jean would take the water and make long sipping sounds. The attention from the listeners gave much joy to Aunt Jean, so she would add a little extra flavor to the story.

"Where was I, child? Were you listening to what I was saying?" She would clap her hands and sing "I'll Fly Away." It was a performance for all to see. She would always ask the same questions and sing the same song before continuing her story.

"Child, the doctor came out while we were in the waiting room and told us that he didn't think that she was going to make it. We all started praying because it looked really bad. All of a sudden we heard your mama scream real loud. It was almost as if we could feel the pain because they ain't had any medicine to stop all that pain! She had been in labor for twenty-four hours, and the poor thing was so tired. But at three o'clock, this little one decided it was time to come on out and greet the world. Your mama had to be attended to around the clock, but she made it through. I tell you, young lady, you almost killed my sister. Baby, I don't mean any harm. We are all glad that you're here and things worked out as they did. Auntie don't mean you any harm, baby, but that is just the truth."

Denise thought about this as she compared her pregnancy to her mother's.

Chapter Thirteen

✤ ✤ ✤

In October, the city's harvest festivals began. Five months had passed since Denise had announced her pregnancy to her family and friends.

There were many mixed emotions regarding Hilton and Denise's pregnancy. Many of them were Denise's thoughts about possibly cursing their unborn child and her lack of faith in God's Word. Denise's Christian walk was sincere, but she depended on others for her faith. Her lack of understanding centered on her apprehensions. In her mind, she felt that her apprehensions were buried in her mother's grave and were beginning to be resurrected by the child in her womb.

Her foolish thoughts lingered as she entered the gates of the Atlanta Federal Penitentiary. Before Bell entered the room, Denise had felt reassured that Bell would give her a Word from God. For three years, Denise had walked closely with God through the life of her husband, Honey, Howard, and Bell. She lived by sight and what others assured her, but not by actual faith in God. She realized that her biggest fear was not the fear of God or the love of God, but of living eternity in hell.

Bell smiled at Denise with joy. Denise knew he had a message from God for her. Bell was the one man, besides her husband, who helped sustained her in her faith. She knew that Bell would help her really believe that all is well and it would be as he spoke it.

"Hello, my dear! Where is Hilton?" Bell sat directly across from Denise.

She shook her head and ran her fingers over her mouth. "He is working today and I—."

"Don't pretend, Denise. You came because you were searching for an answer and you thought I was your answer. You didn't want your loving husband here for the truth of the matter."

"What truth, Bell? I came, as always, to see a friend."

Bell leaned forward, staring in her eyes. "Yes. A friend sticks closer than a brother and that true friend is God. You, my dear, believe that people are your source and not God. God does use people to share the Word, but you have more faith in them than you have in God. You remind me of Jennie."

Denise pushed his hand away. "Please don't compare me to her!"

Bell frowned slightly. "I know she was evil, but you have the same trust factor in people and not God. Jennie believed that her connection with people of power gave her power. Sadly, she also believed that those associates would bring her fame and happiness. You believe that your connection with people who are connected with God will bring you deliverance and not God Himself. You no longer need a priest or pastor to stand before God for you. You can talk directly to God and hear from Him yourself. He will tell you what to do, who to listen to, and confirm what is being taught to you. The Bible says you don't need man to have the anointing and power of God. The problem is that you have a form of godliness. In that form are people like me, Honey, and even your husband. You have not received the Holy Ghost. I know that you don't have to have the anointing to get into heaven, but it will provide you with greater revelation in the power of God."

"Are you saying that I don't believe in God? I do believe in God. I just have some questions regarding this walk. This is nothing like my first introduction to Christ as a child. What you and Honey are saying makes me feel good and gives me hope, but once you stop talking and I return to my life, I lose all hope. Please tell me what you're trying to say. Or are you trying to tell me that I don't really believe."

"Not exactly. I'm saying that your belief is solely based on the faith and relationship of others and not your own relationship with God. The only way you'll get a true understanding is through operating in the Spirit and not in someone else's anointing. You don't have confidence in God for yourself. The only way you'll get that is to truly understand God and the Holy Ghost. Listen carefully to what it says in the Bible. Hebrews 13:5 says God will never leave you. The Book of John says, 'He will send a comforter for you when Jesus leaves, and that comforter is the Holy Spirit.' Stop leaning on others to hear from God. Talk to Him and believe, by faith, that He has already answered your prayers. While you're waiting for that manifestation, continue to pray, read, and mediate on the Word. Get a concordance of the Bible and a Bible dictionary online or in a book. But most of all, get an understanding of the Word by studying yourself. Not Honey's, Hilton's, or my understanding. Have your own relationship with God."

"How do you know all this stuff? Honey said that you knew that Hilton and I were having a baby!"

"Denise, I'm only a vessel for God. I don't know anything on my own. The Spirit of God tells me these things. My discernment comes from God because I have a close relationship with Him. If you want that same gift, make Him your best friend and watch what God will do for you."

"I really want that. I want to be free. I want to be free so bad! Please help me! You said a couple weeks ago that you were freer in prison than I am on the outside. What does that mean?"

"Sweetheart, you don't understand that you're already free. Listen to what I'm saying. God has provided everything that we need. We just have to believe it and walk in it. When Jesus said, 'It is finished!' that means it is done. Learn to listen to God and have peace in Him. I beg of you, let it go and have total healing in God."

Denise held her face in her hands and started to cry. "I don't know how to do that, Bell. How do I get the same relationship with God that you, Hilton, Honey, and Howard have? I'm so afraid that my baby will not live—and I cannot shake that feeling. I can't shake it! I can't seem to let it go. I need a Word from God. Can you tell me if my baby will live?"

"I can tell you that we are already healed because Jesus went to the cross. This is a battle and you have to fight to be healed in Jesus' name. Remember that Matthew 11:12 refers to the violent taking it by force. There is a spiritual war at hand and we must be victorious. Wars are not clean. They are bloody and violent, but we must have a holy passion and determination or we will fail. We have to fight for the prize in this spiritual battle. Remember that God has already given us the victory, but he does give us free will to choose which path we will take. It may not always be easy, but He has overcome every challenge. We have to renew our minds by worshiping God, and reading and studying the Word. If not, we will all perish. We have to fight and strive for the victory in the Spirit realm. If you want your child to live, she will live if you believe that she will live and declare the works of God. She is a seed and cannot fight for herself; we have to fight for her—you and Hilton and all the saints that believe. I personally believe that she will live."

"See? Now I'm more confused than I was before. You just said that God has already given us victory in the battle. Then why do I have to fight? This is so hard!"

"This is kind of hard to explain. God gave you free will to make choices. He also gave you the answer regarding the choices you'll make. He says 'to choose life or death,' but He also says 'choose life.' That life is Jesus, our Savior. Once you choose Him, the Bible says that you'll have trials and tribulations. But don't let your heart be troubled because He has already overcome the world. The Kingdom of Heaven comes by force and passion. We must believe that He has already overcome the world. We know this by studying the Word because faith comes by hearing the Word. Once you hear and obey the Word, your challenges are easy and your victories are His victories. When you hear the Word and obey the Word, you trust and have confidence in God. You don't have to worry because God has your back. You're now resting in Him. Remember you always win with God even if the situation does not end the way you want it to. If you're following God, it will end in God's way. God's way and your way should be the same because you have His Spirit guiding you. Actually, it's rather easy."

"You see, my dear, we have made it hard. Develop an intimate relationship with Him. Fall in love with Him as you have with Hilton. Focus on our Savior and He will take care of you. Let the Holy Spirit work in your life. Does that help you?"

Denise took some tissue out of her purse and wiped her eyes.

"Fall in love like I did with Hilton? I spent a lot of time with Hilton and I did try to find out everything I could. But I was totally in the flesh when I met him. To be honest, I just wanted to sleep with him—until I realized that I didn't want to go to hell. I tried to live my life right because I was afraid that if I died suddenly like Jennie, I might go to hell. I knew I was not living right."

"Denise, don't just be fearful of going to hell, be fearful of hurting God. Not only that, love Him. If you love someone, you'll think twice before doing something that would hurt them. If you love God, you will not want to sin. You would live your life for Him. Not because you're fearful—because you love Him and don't want to hurt Him. You see, Denise, it brings you pleasure to please Him. Pleasing your lover is always rewarding. Our Savior is the lover of our soul, mind, body, and spirit."

"I'll try to learn how to fall in love with God because I want to hear directly from Him," Denise said.

Bell moved toward the security guard at the exit door. "You will—if you trust and follow His plan. I'll see you soon. I have to go. As you know, I'm on penitentiary time. I'm leaving you, but God will never leave you or forsake you. Remember that we fight not against flesh and blood but spirits and principalities in high places. Get to know God in the Spirit."

Denise watched him leave and wondered if she would ever understand a word that he was saying. It was so foreign to her mind, body, and spirit—even after three years of walking with what she thought was God.

Chapter Fourteen

✤ ✤ ✤

TWO WEEKS BEFORE THANKSGIVING, Hilton and Denise selected a menu for the holiday. It was a two-day process based on who was invited and their various requests. Denise's presentation normally added another week to the preparation.

Hilton helped her select the patterns for the table setting. He had little interest in the selection, but he participated to please his pregnant wife. While getting the tablecloths, Denise started to experience severe stomach pains. She could barely make it across the room. Denise sat down and tried to get comfortable. She hoped that the pains would go away, but they continued. She finally had to tell Hilton about them and admit that she had been having them for a while.

"You should have told me so I could have taken you to the doctor a long time ago! Call the doctor right now and let her know we're on our way. I'll go pull around the car!"

Denise told her nurse that she had been feeling a little woozy and was having some pains in her stomach. The nurse said that it was very important to keep tabs on how she was feeling because of her age and the Lupus. She told Denise to come into the office right away. Denise realized that they closed at seven-thirty and it was already seven o'clock.

Hilton grabbed Denise's coat and helped her to the car. The doctor's office was only a couple of minutes away, but the traffic made it feel like it was farther. Dr. Collins had been recommended by Faith and Dr. Williams. She was considered the best in her field. As Hilton was helping Denise out of the car, she noticed that he had a troubled look. He held her hand and led her to the door of the office building.

Hilton said, "I'm sorry if I yelled. You're going to be fine. Trust me. It's going to be okay."

When they got into the office, the nurse asked them to come back to one of the examination rooms. Dr. Collins immediately came into the room and took Denise's blood pressure.

"You need to go to the hospital right now! Your blood pressure is very high and you need to be monitored."

"Wait, wait! Excuse me, doctor. What exactly do you mean? Do I have time to go home and get a couple of things?"

"No! You need to go immediately!"

"I'll go, but I have to be home for Thanksgiving. I'll be having a dinner for my family."

Dr. Collins said, "I don't think you'll be home for Thanksgiving. This is very serious and you need to get to the hospital now."

"Don't worry about Thanksgiving. Let's just be thankful that we are able to get you and the baby to the hospital now. Let's move it, young lady."

Denise's worst nightmare had begun. The same thing that she had done to her mother was happening to her. Her child was killing her. The tears fell and she couldn't stop. "Hilton, why is this happening? I don't understand. I was fine! Please don't allow them to hurt our child!"

"No one will hurt our child. What are you saying? The doctors and the nurses want to help you. Calm down, Denise."

Hilton grabbed Denise by the hand, thanked the doctor, and drove directly to the hospital. A nurse took her blood pressure, administered intravenous drugs, and placed her on a gurney.

Denise screamed as if she was being taken to a death chamber. "Wait! I can't go down the hall! I can't stay here! I have things to do. Please don't hurt my child!"

The nurse said, "I'm sorry, but you'll be staying here tonight. It will be okay. Just relax."

Hilton asked the doctors and nurses about her behavior. The nurse assured him that most pregnant women are emotional, but Hilton sensed that there was more to her behavior. He called Faith and told her about the situation.

Faith happened to be the attending nurse on the next floor. Faith accepted the mother role that was required. She remained at her sister's side for hours in her time of need.

❖ ❖ ❖

The silence of a hospital room was not golden for Denise. At 4:30 in the morning, Denise could still hear a squeaking mop hitting the cold floor, beeping machines, and conversations between the nurses. She held the remote in her right hand, but she had no desire to turn on the TV. She felt that time stood still. Nothing was changing. She would remain captive in this hospital room with her baby growing inside of her. She asked, "When am I leaving? Will my baby live?"

Each doctor, in Denise's mind, gave the same answer, "We'll see," and "We sure hope so." These answers frustrated Denise, especially when she realized that she would be spending Thanksgiving in the hospital. Denise decided to take Bell's advice and read the Word and try to get an understanding of what it was saying. This was the first time she had read it without having Hilton there to explain what it said. She started with the Book of Wisdom; from there, she read the book of John. Before she realized it, she had been reading for hours.

At noon, some unexpected guests knocked on her door. Her family brought a Thanksgiving feast for ten with turkey, dressing, rolls, and all of the fixings: cakes, pies, tablecloths, candles, and all of the trimmings for an elegant holiday feast.

Every item had been prepared by her beloved family members: Faith, Chad, and her niece and nephew. The only thing Denise regretted was that Katie was afraid of her. Denise had so many tubes connected to her that Katie didn't recognize her. It had frightened

Katie to see her aunt looking like a machine. It brought tears to Denise's eyes, but she was determined not to show it.

Faith arranged the tablecloths and candles, although they were not allowed to light them. In spite of that, the setting was beautiful. Just as they were preparing to feast on the meal, Denise got one more surprise guest. She was elated to see Hilton because she thought he had to help his mother and would not be able to visit. As Hilton entered, Denise opened her arms and began to cry.

"I thought I would be alone today," she cried. "But, my family is—"

"Okay! Okay! That's enough," Hilton said as he gave her a kiss. "Let's eat!"

That night as Denise slept, Pastor Bell's voice rang in her ear. "You must release this fear and fight for your child."

The next morning before breakfast was served, Honey entered the room. "My sister, how are you? Have you been resting?"

Denise pulled the covers back to give her a hug. "I've been trying to get an understanding about what is happening to me."

Honey sat on the edge of the bed and gently took her hand. "Denise, I'm not your source of information. You have everything you need. I have a part in your journey, but this is not my hour. Listen to God's voice and repent for anything that is not of God in your heart—no matter how small."

Honey started to talk about her family's Thanksgiving dinner. Denise saw Honey's mouth move, but she didn't hear what she was saying. She was wondering how Honey could be so cold regarding her and her unborn child. This was not the typical Honey. Honey continued to describe Bell's holiday and told her of his well wishes to her and Hilton.

"Denise, did you hear me? Bell sends his love, and he said he will see you soon."

"How can he see me soon? He's in prison and I'm in the hospital. That doesn't make any sense."

"God can take the foolish things to confound the wise. All things are possible with God."

"Honey, I hear you, but I'm so afraid for my child."

"Denise, don't fear! God is with you. Just trust Him at His Word and operate in it!"

Denise could no longer deal with the guilt she felt for cursing her unborn child. She had no choice but to be honest and seek help from those who had the knowledge of God.

"Honey, I never even told Hilton what I'm about to tell you. You see, my aunt told me that my mom had a challenging pregnancy with me. She was never the same and later died. My birth killed her, and now my child is killing me."

"Denise, do you recall the teachings on speaking the Word in the atmosphere and not speaking death? You're declaring curses with your own words. Don't ever say what you just said again to anyone. Don't even think it—do you hear me? You must replace those thoughts with the Word of God. The Bible says that there are blessings and curses. Go through your Bible and find scriptures on blessings. I want you to confess the blessings and forsake those thoughts. Ask God for forgiveness for what you have been thinking and saying. Tell God that you're sorry for the thoughts of death and confusion. Pray to Him saying, 'I know that you're not a God of confusion. I forsake those thoughts and replace them with your Word. Father, you have given us life! I understand that life and death are in the power of the tongue as your Holy Word says. I choose to speak life! Your Words are life and spirit.' Denise, make your confession personal to God."

"Is that all I have to do? That seems so simple."

Denise repeated Honey's prayer of confession. Honey listened to her attentively.

"Denise, that is not all you have to do. You must believe it until those words become life to your soul. You have to arrive at the point where God's words are more real to you than this actual physical world. At that point, nothing will matter to you but your Father and His will. That, my dear, is walking in the Spirit. You'll not be troubled, shaken, or moved by anything because you'll know that you know that God is your protector and shield. Reading and studying the Word brings honor and favor that you cannot imagine. Miracles will happen in your life and everything that you think or desire will be given to you because He loves you. In essence, take care of His business and He will take care of yours. Seek His face and not His hand. Just fall in love with Him."

"That's the same thing that Bell said."

"You see, my dear, we can pray for you until the hogs come home, but if you don't believe and you speak against what we are all praying, then it's all in vain. You're hindering the blessings of God with your unbelief and lack of faith. As I prayed for you in the Spirit, it was revealed to me that you have the spirit of unforgiveness in your heart. Unforgiveness, along with your unbelief, will stop any healing or blessing. Please find truth and freedom in our loving God. Where the Spirit is, there is liberty."

"Is that why you're so calm about my situation? You believe that I have to choose to believe God basically at His Word—and that Word has to become real to me?"

"Denise, read God's Word and find out the mysteries and the treasures of God. It's so sweet. Money cannot buy this, and I cannot really explain it to you. You must experience it for yourself. I can try to explain it to you all day long, but without the Holy Spirit living inside of you, you cannot fully understand it. If you want to live, you better figure it out and do it quickly. Don't just read the Word—mediate on the scriptures, let it saturate your heart. Feel the depths of the words and understand the meaning of the scriptures you are reading. On that note, my dear, I must leave. I have another friend to visit. I'll see you later."

Honey kissed Denise's cheek and wished her God's best.

As Honey departed, Denise reflected on her words. How could Honey be so cruel and direct to someone in the hospital, especially when they are facing a life-and-death situation? Is this what she meant by God's words piercing the heart and soul in her teaching of the Word? Honey's words pierced Denise's heart and it hurt. Honey's language belonged to another person and was not the usual conversation between her and Denise. How could she ever be at the point that Hilton, Honey, and Howard were with God? That would take years and she only had three months before she delivered her baby. None of what Honey said made sense, especially when there had not been any changes in her health and pregnancy. Denise's prayers were not being answered and no one could help her. She realized that she would have to help herself.

Denise began to cry out to God from her hospital bed. As the tears flowed down her face, her heart was disappointed. She didn't see any change or manifestation of healing in her body. Nurses and the lab techs entered the room throughout the night because of her constant crying. Their concern for her was touching, but it didn't help her. Denise would not eat anything for twenty-four hours and was given liquids. Denise was so tired she could not tell if she was dreaming or starting to see things.

At 5:30 am, she saw a pearl cross forming in the television set. But the set was not turned on. The cross changed into a dove and flew out of the television. It stared at her for a moment, and then she saw what appeared to be a transparent giant beside her bed. She could not tell if it was a man or a woman, but she was not afraid of the being. There was so much love that Denise felt a love for mankind and an overwhelming peace. The transparent being didn't speak. Denise realized that she was in the presence of an angel from God. Suddenly a voice came out of nowhere. The voice was like no other that she had ever heard.

"My child, don't cry, for I'm with you and will be with you always."

The voice reassured her that He knew that she had not killed her mother. Her mother was at peace and she didn't need to worry about her. Her time on earth must be spent on the things of God and not on the past.

"You must forget the things of the past and focus on the things to come. Come, arise, and let me show you what is to come."

Denise rose out of her body to a place that she had never been. She looked down and could see herself on her bed. The figure remained near her bedside. She entered into a time that she knew was yet to come. It was a wonderful home with three children and a loving husband. Hilton was teaching the Word of God to her children! She could even see herself preparing for others to come.

Hilton told the children that they were a legacy and must listen to be prepared to teach to others what was being taught to them.

"You see, my child, you're carrying a legacy for me and my kingdom. You and your husband will pastor and preach the Word to my flock until I come back. Please understand that my words will never return to me empty. It's important that you believe my Word and my promises for the life and the legacy of your children—and the people that you and your generation are called to save. Look behind you, my child. What do you see?"

As she looked back, she saw millions of people worshiping God. Denise and her entire family were standing before them. She turned to her right and saw Bell in his prison cell—on his knees praying for her and her unborn child. In the distance, Honey, Howard, and Hilton were in prayer with Faith and Chad. They were all praying for the birth of her child and her healing. They were thanking God for their healing and worshiping Him.

The Voice of God said, "The prayers of my righteous avail much, my child. Please understand that the just shall live by faith. Have faith in me and see my glory. Don't lose sight of my promises. I have given you the victory."

Denise was awakened by a light knock at the door at 8:30. Dr. Brewster asked if Hilton was in the hospital. She had been sleeping for hours and felt refreshed. She pondered the dream as her visitor entered the room.

"Why do you need my husband? I'm fine. I just had a little talk with God."

"That's all well and good. Two or three heads are better than one. Have you urinated lately?" he asked as he looked at her catheter bag.

"Not a lot, but I know that it will improve soon. The levels on the bag are small."

"Young lady, you and your baby are not well! I have some concerns regarding your state."

"What state might that be? You see, doctor, I had some concerns, too. But now I'm sure that all is well!"

"I'm not so sure about that, young lady."

Dr. Brewster, an obstetrics and gynecology specialist, was mystified by Denise's condition. He wanted desperately to be a part of her recovery team. A graduate of Howard Medical School and the son of a prominent surgeon in New York, he wanted to stand on his own. He knew that the successful delivery and recovery of Denise and her baby would be the ideal medical study. Denise's medical condition opened the door for validation within the medical community and his father's heart. This would create success for his name. He flipped through Denise's chart: a thirty-three-year-old pregnant black female with Systemic Lupus Erythematosus, maternal hypertension, alopecia, mucosal ulcer, rheumatoid arthritis, potential liver failure, and renal disease. Dr. Brewster had listed the prognosis as fatal in his November 27, 2007, notation in the chart. Dr. Brewster knew he needed a miracle to save his prize patient. Two days after his first notation, Denise's condition started to get worse—and it appeared hopeless. Dr. Brewster had decided that an immediate C-section could save Denise's life. He didn't know if there was any hope for the baby.

Denise's body was stiff and sore. She attempted to look in Dr. Brewster's eyes.

"I'm fine. My husband will be here within the hour."

"That will be great." He glanced at his watch. "We should call him and ask him to come a little sooner and—"

"I'd be happy to call him, but all is well. I'm healed by the Lord!"

"That is nice," Dr. Brewster said while noting in the chart that the patient was in denial and needed a psychiatric evaluation. "I would like speak to both of you as soon as possible about the baby. Please bear with me, Mrs. Johnson."

"Dr. Brewster, I understand that you must do your part and God will do the rest. But as I said before, all is well. Why do you have that look of disbelief? You don't believe that—."

To Denise's surprise, Hilton walked in with a smile that could light up any room. "How is my sweetie?" Hilton kissed Denise's forehead.

"I'm good. As a matter of fact, I'm healed by the Lord."

"You do sound happy and well. You even look better."

Dr. Brewster grabbed a chair and said, "I'm pleased to meet you, Mr. Johnson. I'm Dr. Brewster. Have a seat, Mr. Johnson. We were just speaking about you. We need to discuss Denise and the baby."

"It's a pleasure to meet you, sir." Hilton extended his hand.

Denise, beaming with excitement said, "Hilton, I have so much to tell you! Dr. Brewster would not speak to me without you here. He doesn't believe me when I tell him that all is well! I'm healed!"

"Sweetie, you believe you are healed? I've been waiting for so long for you to say it like you mean it!"

"Hilton, I must tell you about my dream. I saw you praying with everybody last night. Were you praying with Honey and Howard last night?"

"Yes! Yes! We were all standing in agreement and praying for healing for our family!"

"Hilton, I believe! I can shout it on the rooftop that God is real! He came into my room! He came in my room! It was not a dream—it was real!"

Dr. Brewster cleared his throat and said, "Excuse me! But I have other patients. Do you mind? I really need to speak to both of you."

Hilton chuckled and stepped toward Dr. Brewster. "I'm so sorry, Dr. Brewster, if we confused you. We just had a major breakthrough in faith. So no matter what you say, it is well."

He looked at Hilton and silently asked for patience. "Yes, of course. This is somewhat complex and I wanted both of you to hear the details together in case you had any questions."

Dr. Brewster slowly walked to the window. "I need you to discuss the options that I'm about to present to you. As you both know, we are running out of time. Since my last visit, the situation has become critical. I indicated to Denise that we would have to make some major decisions if her condition didn't improve with the medication."

"Is this the day the rubber meets the road, Dr. Brewster?" Hilton asked.

"It could be worse. Let me explain."

Dr. Brewster summarized Denise's and the baby's medical condition. He had gone through the options with Denise's Lupus specialist. Knowing that this was not a planned pregnancy due to Denise's recent diagnosis, Dr. Brewster understood that there were many other complications. Baby Johnson had caused a lot of stress to Denise's body. As the baby grew, the stress on her fragile body was increasing. Dr. Brewster strongly recommended an immediate C-section. Denise and Hilton were not surprised by the doctor's recommendation, but they felt that they needed some additional time to think about it.

Dr. Brewster emphatically stated that there was no more time. Denise was having liver and kidney failure. The decision needed to be made within the next two hours. Denise watched carefully as Dr. Brewster placed the handwritten medical recommendation on her nightstand. Dr. Brewster didn't want to rush them, but he needed an answer immediately. He realized that the baby was nearly six months in utero and the chance for survival was low. It was either Denise or the baby—and he wanted to save them both. The fact that Denise was not concerned puzzled him—surely she was in denial.

"Do we need to sign these papers?" Hilton asked.

"No. I just want you to look over the documents and read about your options. I'm going to give you some time alone. I'll be back within the hour to check in with you. You must make a decision immediately."

Dr. Brewster extended his hand to Hilton. "Call me if you have any questions." He stopped at the door. "Remember, it's imperative that we have the decision today."

Denise shared her encounter with God to Hilton. She radiated as she spoke of the vision and the voice of God and how much love she felt in His presence. The vision had given her a hope that she had never had before and she understood what Hilton and everyone else was describing. Denise's energy and faith were bold and confident. She was a new person with an entirely different perspective regarding her health and the health of her child. This sudden change pleased Hilton and he prayed that it was not temporary.

Denise said, "He is real! He is real and He loves us all!"

"Hilton, our child will live and she will declare the works of the Lord!" Denise screamed at the top of her lungs.

"I'm so excited, Denise, that you believe. I just hope this is not a momentary change."

"I believe and understand God for myself! He is real and I know that we will have this child and two more! I don't care if you believe me or not. It doesn't matter what you know. I know and God knows my heart. Believe whatever you want because I'm finally free. Do you hear me, Hilton Lamar Johnson? I'm free!"

"Now that's what I'm talking about! Baby, you said that with boldness, confidence, and power! Now that you believe and we are in agreement with God's word, miracles will occur because we share in His word. We have been fasting and praying for a breakthrough for you. When we prayed in tongues, it was confirmed that you had unforgiveness and unbelief. You were blocking your own healing and it was killing our unborn child. I'm so grateful that you prayed, fasted, and were led to seek Him for yourself. God's anointing can heal and do anything according to His will and plan for your life. And He will get the glory. I truly understand that His ways are not our ways because He could have just healed you and our child in a blink of an eye. He wanted you to see something. He is amazing!"

"Yes, He is truly amazing. I really cannot tell you how much."

Hilton and Denise shared their faith as a couple for a while, speaking of God's goodness and love. They examined the Word for their baby and prayed until Dr. Brewster returned to the room for their decision.

Denise and Hilton could hear Dr. Brewster laughing with his staff in the hallway. Dr. Brewster entered the room and said, "You look even better than you did earlier. You're showing signs of improvement, but there are still some problems." He tilted his head to the read the monitors.

"There'll always be problems, Dr. Brewster, as long as I have good insurance," Denise said with a giggle.

"I don't know about that. But I do know one thing, Mrs. Johnson, as long as your insurance is in effect, we will treat you." Dr.

Brewster laughed with her. "What is this I hear about you keeping up all of this noise?"

"That's not me, doctor. That would be my rude husband."

"Let's not be so hasty to blame everything on your husband. So what is your decision?"

"Is it still necessary?" Denise asked. "You said that I was doing better and you saw some improvement."

"Calm down. You seem to be doing better, but there are still some problems, and we must deliver the baby soon. That has not changed."

Denise listened attentively, but she believed that she would be out of the hospital soon.

"Hilton and I have agreed to go ahead with the surgery and trust God. We both know that this is for His purpose."

Chapter Fifteen

✤ ✤ ✤

THAT NIGHT, DENISE DELIVERED a baby girl. Two weeks after the birth, they named her Holly. Denise and Holly were both recovering slowly. Holly's body was extremely small and fragile. The tiny baby could be carried in the palm of the hands of the nurses and doctors who were attending to her. In spite of Holly's appearance, Hilton was rejoicing over the birth of his daughter and the healing of his wife. He brought his family and friends to see his little girl with great pride.

As Denise's healing progressed, she waited anxiously to see Holly. She had not been able to hold her since the birth. On December 3, Denise received two great gifts from God. She would be allowed to see and hold her beautiful daughter. Hilton arrived at the hospital with a bouquet of flowers for Denise. He also brought family and friends to share this special moment. Of course, Minnie, Uncle Ed, Aunt Frances, Honey, and Howard were there. As he entered the room, he kissed his loving wife and gave her the flowers. He was followed by a host of supportive family and friends. Laughter filled the room when another guest arrived.

Denise screamed. She could not believe who was standing in her presence—dressed in a nice suit and newly shaved. "Is this a dream? Is it real?" She held out her arms and embraced the most welcomed visitor. "I cannot believe this! How did this happen?"

"Yes! To God be the glory! Sergeant Johnson was working for another drug lord and planted information on me and others. He was sent to prison and all of his cases were thrown out of court. I was given credit for the time served. All I have to do is pay the IRS what I owe them, but I'm as free as you are!"

"This is truly a wonderful day!" Denise said as she hugged Bell. "Let's all go down and see our child."

Hilton pushed Denise in a wheelchair toward Holly's room. They looked like an army marching down a battlefield. They had won the battle, but the war was not over.

As they approached Holly's room, a nurse asked. "Are you Holly's parents?"

"Yes!" Hilton answered.

"Please follow me," said the nurse. "The rest of you will have to remain outside of the room."

It was obvious to the others that something was wrong and they needed to pray. They joined hands and Howard led them in prayer. While they were praying, Hilton and Denise were given the shocking news that Holly had passed on to glory.

"I don't understand!" Denise said. "God promised me that Holly would live and I'm still standing on what He said! I know that His Word will never return to Him void. He promised me! But I believe, and he will do what His Word says."

Hilton held his wife and embraced her like never before. "You're right, my dear. She will live and declare the works of God. Where is my daughter? Don't move her before we pray over her!"

The nurse agreed to their wishes because Holly had just passed away.

Hilton and Denise returned to the lobby and told their loved ones that Holly had passed away. They stood in agreement with them through prayer as Hilton and Denise laid hands on Holly. As they approached the room, the nurse gave her condolences to the family.

Hilton replied, "Thank you, but God will get the glory."

Hilton guided Denise toward the small bed. Suddenly, Denise had the strength to stand on her own. Hilton and Denise laid their hands on Holly's lifeless body. The others extended their hands toward them while they prayed.

Hilton said, "I declare, in the name of Jesus, that you are healed. He sent His Word and delivered you from destruction. Jesus, your Word is Yes and Amen, and it will never return void. I declare and decree on this day that Holly Johnson will live and declare the works of the Lord."

Suddenly Holly gasped for breath and started moving her little head. She opened her eyes and looked directly at her parents. The nurse screamed, ran out of the room, and called the doctors. The medical team arrived and was in shock to see the baby that they had pronounced dead an hour earlier was alive. They took her vitals and gave her a complete examination. To their surprise, they declared that Holly was completely well. They could not explain to Denise and Hilton what had happened or how it was possible that Holly was alive. Denise smiled, looked into the eyes of the doctors, and said, "It was the honey in the rock—the sweet Holy Spirit working in us for the rock of God.

"To God be the glory for this day and forever more," said Bell with his hands lifted to the heavens.

Biblical References

❖ ❖ ❖

www.BibleGateway.com
www.ChimainDouglasMinistries.com